# FALLEN EMBERS

M. L. Scarberry

Pretty Punk
Publishing

Fallen Embers



This book is a work of fiction. Any reference to historical events, real people, or real places are used fictitiously. Other names, characters, places, and events are products of the author's imagination, and any resemblance to actual events or places or persons, living or dead, is entirely coincidental.

Printed in the United States of America

Cover design by: TheAuthorAtlier

Book formatting by: ArtfulDigitalDloads

First printed in 2024

ISBN: 979-8-9914157-0-5

*For Brad and Mikala,*

*who encouraged me to light the fire.*

Dear Readers,

Thank you so much for picking up *Fallen Embers*. I'm thrilled to share this story with you, and I'd like to take a moment to introduce myself.

I'm a wife and a proud mom to a little girl who inspires me every day. As a parent on this journey, one of my deepest goals is to create stories that I would be proud for her to read when she's old enough. With that in mind, *Fallen Embers* is written for readers aged 15 and up. This novel explores themes of romantic relationships, the battle between good and evil, redemption, revenge, and violence, all interwoven with religious elements. While it's a work of fiction, these themes are powerful and should be approached with care and thoughtfulness.

Writing and publishing a novel has been a dream of mine since I was a little girl. Back then, I could only imagine what it would feel like to hold my own book in my hands, but today, I'm living proof that dreams can become a reality.

We live in a time where telling your story is more achievable than ever, with countless platforms and opportunities available to help bring your words to life. It's never too soon or too late to begin, so if you have a story inside you, I encourage you to write it, nurture it, and share it—you never know whose heart it might touch.

Lastly, I'd love to hear from you! Whether you have thoughts about the book, questions, or just want to share your own dreams, please don't hesitate to reach out. Your feedback and stories mean the world to me.

MichelleLeeScarberry@gmail.com

Thank you for joining me on this journey. I hope you find something in *Fallen Embers* that resonates with you.

Happy Reading,

M. L. Scarberry

# CHAPTER ONE

## DEMON

Finn dragged his feet through the corridors of Hell. He was in no hurry to see Soren. As a demon, being summoned by his boss was never a good thing, and at least one hundred years had passed since their last encounter.

As he approached the office, walls of fire cast eerie, shifting shadows across the sign on the door. *Infernal Emissary,* it read. Beneath it, in smaller writing: *Enforcer of Contracts, and Management of Affairs Relating to the Souls of the Damned.*

Finn combed a hand through his long, auburn hair, sweeping it away from his crimson eyes. He took a deep breath to calm his nerves. His heart pounded as he raised his hand, but before he could knock, the door swung open. He stepped back from the doorway, but his presence was already known as a chilling voice cut through the air. "Ah, Finneas. Come in."

As Finn entered, he couldn't help but feel the weight of Soren's authority pressing down on him. This wasn't just an office; it was a throne room. A place where decisions of immense consequences were made. The room was vast, with high ceilings that disappeared into the shadows, giving the impression of an endless cavern.

Rich tapestries hung between huge iron sconces on the wall, their fires casting long, glowing reflections that danced and twisted across the polished marble floor. In the center of the room was a large obsidian desk on a grand pedestal, carved with ornate runes and demonic faces, which followed Finn as he approached. Soren sat behind the desk, his presence amplified by the desk's elevated position. His shrouded form was illuminated on the desk's mirror-like surface by the flickering flames surrounding him. Finn held his composure, though anxiety gnawed at him from within. "You wanted to see me?"

Soren's piercing black eyes bore into him from under his dark cloak. He sat up, a long growl leaving his throat before he spoke down to Finn. "Your recent endeavors on Earth have left much to be desired. I had our Overseer, Morvina, pull your file, and it turns out..." Soren tossed an overstuffed manila folder down at Finn's feet. The name *Finneas Ignautus* was stamped in red letters across the front. "Your failures are becoming quite the collection."

Finn's lips formed a sarcastic smile as he attempted to keep his voice steady. "Well, it's not easy causing chaos when humans are so good at doing it themselves. I feel like I should be taking notes from them."

Soren's deep growl pulsated through the office, which made the flickering light around him blaze with intensity. "Your insolence is testing my patience, Finneas. I've given you ample opportunities over the last century, and yet your incompetence persists."

"I do try to be persistent." Finn managed a small laugh but quickly cleared his throat and looked down at the scattered papers at his feet, their edges singed and glowing. "So, I take it, you have another assignment for me, then?"

"I have a *final* opportunity. Something so simple even you won't be able to botch it." Soren leaned back, the flames around him dying down into a flicker once more. A wicked smile stretched across his scaly, burned skin, barely visible under the dark cloak he was wearing. "You've been put on *high-alert*, Finneas. Do you know what that means for you?"

Finn raised his red eyes to meet Soren's gaze. "I'm guessing I won't be invited to the company picnic?"

"It means," Soren's voice was growing louder again, "that if you somehow manage to fail again, even the lowest depths of Hell will no longer welcome you, *and* you'll bypass any chance at the work prison. You were never a demon to begin with—you've already been expelled by your creator, not surprisingly. Mess up again and you'll get to see how far your sarcasm will get you when Earth is the only place you have left to go."

Finn clenched his jaw. Expulsion. The very thought of being banished again turned his stomach. Being shunned by both realms was a bleak existence he couldn't face. This was his last chance to reignite his demonic nature, and evade the fate that threatened to strip him of everything he knew. A chance to prove that he belonged in the underworld. Finn's expression hardened as he looked at his boss head-on. "Whatever it is, I'll take care of it."

"A simple task," Soren said calmly, interlocking his fingers, which were hidden beneath black, leathery gloves. "You'll be doing what you were supposed to be doing all along—collecting a soul and bringing it back. Here is the location." Soren tossed a small card on top of the file at Finn's feet. "You'll go there, use fire to end the mortal's life, collect the soul, and bring it to our Intake Department. If you succeed, no more *high-alert*."

Finn picked up the card and studied it. The front displayed only a picture of a door. A green apartment door with the numbers 111 on it. "Who lives here?" he asked.

"Just a mortal girl, Finneas, nobody of importance. This job would typically be reserved for an agent, and although they have been working overtime, the other side claimed the souls of her parents only a year ago. We need to get to her before they do. I'm sure you understand, quotas being what they are."

"And why fire? That seems to draw a lot of *attention*."

Soren's laughter startled Finn as it echoed throughout the office. "Why not? Fire is within you. Don't pretend it isn't. If you weren't such a failure this whole time, you'd be the embodiment of Hell, itself."

Finn hid his crimson eyes by closing them tightly. It wasn't always the case, but fire coursed through his veins, and now he would be using it to extinguish a life. Seeing Finn's reluctance, Soren continued. "A quick death is too easy. This requires something a little more *dramatic.* You need to show me you really deserve to be here, or if you're just another failure meant to cast away."

A heavy silence settled between them. Finn's chest tightened, a surge of unease flooding him. He had certainly done some questionable things during his 6000 years of existence, but killing an innocent girl?

The line between good and evil was usually blurred with Finn. His best friend, an angel named Owlen, had always been the voice of reason in times like this. Like Finn, Owlen was ejected from Heaven. But while Finn aspired to make a name for himself as a demon, Owlen's pursuits have always been rooted in good. *Pure and good.* Finn had always admired him for that, although he never said so.

His red eyes bore the weight of the internal struggle—a silent battle between his loyalty to Hell, and the undeniable influence of Owlen. Ultimately, the prospect of failure and external exile once again was a prospect he couldn't ignore. "Consider it done," he muttered.

"Good," Soren nodded. "I knew you'd be more than grateful to take this assignment. And who knows, if you can turn things in the right direction, you may be working as an agent soon enough."

The door Finn had walked through had once again opened, and he was glad to make his exit. Holding the card tightly, he didn't look back, but heard the distant rumble of Soren's voice behind him. "Don't disappoint me."

As Finn trudged through the twisting hallways, his eyes glowed with a radiance against the darkness, marking him apart from the shadowy creatures that clung to every corner. Those eyes, usually a symbol of his defiance and wit, now carried the weight of uncertainty as he stood at the hazy portal between realms. He stepped through and emerged from the other side, seamlessly.

Pedestrians hurried along the bustling sidewalks, too busy to notice the figure that just appeared before them. His appearance was a balance between blending in and standing out. His flowing auburn hair and red eyes made him distinctive, while his choice of attire allowed him to blend into the urban landscape. A fitted black t-shirt clung to his lean frame, accentuating the muscles beneath, while dark jeans hugged his legs as he walked, giving way to a pair of tall, black combat boots.

Concealed from mortal eyes were a pair of magnificent wings that stretched to his feet when unfurled. They lay invisible against his back, selectively unveiled only when circumstances demanded. In times of danger or when he needed to assert dominance, he could summon his wings with a mere thought. They were a constant reminder of who he was and the journey he had undertaken—no longer the ivory white they had been during his creation. As a fallen angel venturing into the darkness of Hell, his shimmery feathers shifted to a deep, obsidian black with smoldering embers at the tips. When they materialized, their shadowy span was a symbol of his past and the dark choices he made.

Finn made his way through the crowded streets. The aroma of hot dogs from a food vendor filled the air, mixed with the occasional scent of car exhaust. Pigeons flapped and cooed around the feet of passersby, scavenging for crumbs. He slipped his way through the sea of faces, going unnoticed, looking for a quieter street.

As he walked toward a secluded alley, a familiar presence suddenly appeared at his side. Finn turned to see Owlen standing there, dressed impeccably in his signature white ensemble. His coat was pristine, tailored to perfection, while his vest was buttoned neatly over his slightly rounded belly. His golden hair was perfectly in place, catching the sunlight like a halo.

Owlen looked at Finn, his beautiful blue eyes revealing a mix of curiosity and concern. "Finneas, my dear friend, we haven't met in the city in decades. What brings you to this neck of the woods?" Owlen inquired. His voice was a blend of genuine interest and underlying worry.

"Finn, angel. It's *Finn*. Do you want me to go around calling you *Owlennean*?"

Owlen blushed slightly. "I'd love that, thank you."

"Not going to happen," Finn said, dismissing such formalities. He leaned against a lamppost, gazing down at their shadows in the afternoon sun—his tall and slender, Owlen's shorter and slightly plump. "It's a bit of a delicate matter. Got an assignment from downstairs, that's all. Nothing major, just a little *task* I'm supposed to carry out." He paused to gauge Owlen's reaction, hoping he wouldn't pry.

Owlen furrowed his brow slightly. "An assignment from *downstairs*? You mean an order from Soren?" His voice dropped a bit, his concern deepening. "Finn, you know how I feel about all that."

Finn nodded, a conflicting expression flickering across his features. "Yeah, I know, but I have my reasons this time. Just trust me, alright?" He glanced away, concealing any trace of pain Owlen may see in his eyes.

Owlen placed his hand on Finn's shoulder. "You're treading a dangerous path with Soren. How many times do I have to tell you that I know deep down this isn't you? You've got goodness in you, despite your... afflictions."

Finn's lips twitched into something resembling a smile. "Afflictions, huh? Well I wouldn't be much of a demon without those, would I?" His gaze met Owlen's blue eyes with a mix of fondness and regret. "Listen, it's complicated, but this job is one I need to do. I won't risk the consequences of failing this time."

Owlen's expression fell. He looked heartbroken, like he was watching a dear friend make a decision that pained him greatly.

As if he were reading Owlen's thoughts, Finn sighed. "It's not that simple. You know who I am. You've known for ages."

"I do know, Finn. But I also know you are capable of so much more than this. You're capable of love and creation." He stepped closer, his voice lowering to almost a whisper. "Remember *Luminara*?"

Memories surged forth of the tiny, secret planet they conjured by their combined powers, before they were exiled. A beautiful place with a quaint forest, streams—it was a sanctuary where they could meet outside of the constraints of judgment.

For many years, the two of them found solace on their hidden planet, away from the prying eyes of others. Sometimes they would just sit in companionable silence, the weight of their cosmic responsibilities momentarily lifted. Other times, they engaged in endless debates about the purpose of creation, or whether the intentions of their creator were really as they seemed. Their shared doubts forged their camaraderie against the celestial realm that would ultimately lead to their banishment.

Owlen named it, of course. Luminara. He has always been sentimental. The name was a testament to the love and friendship that flourished there. After their fateful expulsion, the two began to only meet in secluded corners of reality on Earth. With his heart now heavy with resentment and bitterness, Finn couldn't bring himself to revisit the paradise they created.

Owlen, however, traveled there often. Although alone in his pilgrimage, the planet's serenity reminded him of the gentle spirit that had initially drawn him to Finn. With each visit, he continued to transform their place into a mesmerizing tapestry of wonder. Every corner was adorned with his imagination, and desire to infuse everything with goodness and beauty. Their visits and non-visits spoke to the different paths they had walked since the fall. While it was a place of remembrance and dedication for Owlen, Finn's deliberate avoidance of the planet had allowed him to gradually push it into the recesses of his memory—until now.

For a moment, Finn's defenses seemed to crumble. "I remember." He leaned into Owlen's touch, his eyes closing as if savoring the fleeting comfort. But then, with a heavy sigh, he straightened up, his expression a mixture of resolve and regret. "I appreciate the concern, angel, but I made my choice." He met Owlen's gaze, his eyes pained, yet determined. "I'm seeing this one through."

Owlen's shoulders sagged, his hand dropping at his side. He looked at Finn with both sadness and resignation. "Very well, then. If it's what you really want. I can't risk you hating me, so I won't stand in your way." He took a step back, his eyes holding a hint of lingering hope. He straightened his white ensemble and swept his golden hair into place. "Just remember, you know where to find me if you change your mind."

Finn's gaze flickered with emotion as he watched Owlen step away and disappear from sight, leaving him alone by the quiet alley. "Yeah, I know," he said to the empty space where

Owlen just stood. He wished he could have said something to express the inner turmoil that churned within him.

He knew Owlen would have done anything to make things right. But he also knew that his intervention would veer him away from what must be done. And so, he clung to the unsaid, finding strange comfort in protecting Owlen from the painful truth of what he was about to do.

Finn was several blocks from the address he had been given. While instant traveling is the preferred method of transit for demons and angels alike—allowing them to swiftly and effortlessly move through realms and across physical spaces —he began to walk instead. It was as if the very act of delaying his arrival might somehow offer relief from the inevitable. Yet with each deliberate step he took, any hope for that relief was fleeting.

His keen gaze picked out several other demons blending in with the human crowd, unnoticed by those around them. Their expressions were cool and devoid of emotion as they followed their targets.

Finn watched one demon—a sharp-dressed businessman, who on the surface appeared as any other. He stalked a young man engrossed in his phone, completely unaware that he would meet his end before the day was through.

These demons didn't have complications. They didn't have an angel's voice echoing in their mind, making them question their every move. They simply executed their orders, leaving a trail of ruined lives in their wake—and for a moment, Finn envied them.

He shifted his thoughts to the unavoidable encounter ahead, leaving the other demons to their grim work. But little did he know that as he made his way to apartment number 111, the very fabric of his demonic existence was about to unravel, and would set into motion a series of events that he could not foresee.

# CHAPTER TWO

## MORTAL

Scarlett walked toward the checkout counter at Mason's Hardware, her arms full of painting supplies. As she approached, she noticed the old man behind the counter pressing buttons and fidgeting with the cash register, a look of frustration on his face.

"I'm sorry, miss," he said, looking up at her with a sheepish expression. "This darn thing seems to have jammed."

"It's okay," Scarlett replied with a warm smile. "I'm not in a hurry." Her brown eyes sparkled with kindness. She set her items on the counter, feeling relieved to get a break from holding them. She would have to carry everything three blocks away to her apartment, and the supplies were starting to feel heavy in her arms.

The old man returned her smile, appreciating her patience, and continued to fiddle with the cash register, trying to repair it. Scarlett waited patiently as a few more customers formed a line behind her. The old man jiggled the drawer and pressed more buttons, his hands shaking nervously.

She glanced down at her wrist and removed the ponytail elastic she had placed there the night before, working her long brown hair into a braid. She rubbed the indentation left behind by the elastic, and a dull ache formed in her chest. Her silver bracelet usually hung from that wrist, and it had been missing since she began packing boxes to move from her parents' house.

The drawer shut with a snap, pulling Scarlett from her thoughts. "Got it, miss. Sorry for the wait," he said with a relieved smile. "Will you be needing any paint mixed today?"

"That's okay," she said, her voice warm and understanding. "This is it. I already have paint." She handed over the items for him to scan. He rang up each item with his shaky hands and placed them carefully into bags.

"Thanks, again, miss. Come back soon, now," the old man said, handing her two large bags over the counter.

"I will," she said, adjusting the heavy bags on her arm. The bell above the door rang loudly as she made her exit and began to walk home.

Scarlett pushed open the door of her apartment and dropped the bags in the middle of the living room with a sigh of relief, feeling the strain lift from her muscles. The empty apartment was stark and uninviting, its walls bare and cold. In the corner, a can of purple paint sat waiting for her on top of some newspaper. Just a few years earlier, her mom used the paint to redecorate Scarlett's bedroom at their family home, and now, she hoped it would infuse this space with a sense of hope and healing. It would be a welcome change after the events that brought her here. This new apartment was her chance to start over—an opportunity for a fresh beginning after her world fell apart just a year ago.

Her gaze fell upon a picture frame lying on the floor in front of the makeshift mantel. She created the mantel by repurposing an old bookshelf—which she figured must have wobbled, causing the frame to fall off while she was gone. The glass was broken, lying in a pile of shards underneath, but luckily, the photo was unharmed. She walked over to the frame and picked it up. *Parker Family Christmas 2019* was engraved into the wood. It captured a moment of pure joy— her parents standing behind her in their goofy, matching Christmas sweaters, their arms wrapped tightly around her. Her eyes misted as she traced the contours of their faces with her fingers. Their deaths came suddenly that following spring. The virus that had already taken the lives of dozens of others in town, had taken theirs too, leaving Scarlett alone to pick up the pieces.

Sunlight filtered through the window, casting warm beams onto a stack of moving boxes in the corner. These were the only remaining boxes to be unpacked. They were full of the only belongings not donated after her parents' deaths—reminders of the past that she wasn't ready to confront.

As she placed the photograph back onto the mantel, the sunlight reflected off of something silver on the floor, surrounded by dust. Scarlett's breath caught in her throat as she rushed to pick it up. The bracelet that she thought was lost forever was now found, its chain broken. She pulled it to her chest in a tiny embrace, relieved to see it again. She turned it over to read it, just as she had done every day since receiving it as a gift during the last Christmas with her parents. *Letti, We Love You* was engraved on the front of the delicate nameplate, covered in dirt.

Letti was what they called her, and she much preferred it to Scarlett when she was a child. Sometimes she could hear her mother's voice echoing in the corners of her mind. *Letti Spaghetti,* she would say—a nod to Scarlett's slender frame as well and her mother's silly way of rhyming everything.

Scarlett opened her small toolbox, which was already in use from removing outlet covers the day before. She pulled out a pair of needle nose pliers, and worked carefully to repair the broken link on the bracelet, making it wearable again. She put the bracelet on and wrapped her hand around it, sighing with relief to have it back on her wrist.

She made her way to the bathroom, and flipped on the light, illuminating the small, unfinished space. The faucet creaked slightly as she turned it on, and cold water spurted from the tap. Holding the delicate bracelet under the stream, she watched as the water gradually washed away the dirt from the silver. She glanced at her reflection in the mirror as water began to swirl down the drain.

At nineteen, she was the spitting image of her mother, and she found herself avoiding the bathroom mirror more and more lately. If she looked into her brown eyes long enough, she could see her mother looking back, and it was too painful. As the cool water flowed freely over her hands, her mind became lost in thought. The sound of the faucet was a gentle hum in the background, blending with her memories, and as she stood there gently tracing the intricate words on her bracelet beneath the water, she was wholly unaware of the presence that lingered just beyond her front door.

Finn stood before the green door of apartment number 111. His mind was a hailstorm of conflicting thoughts and emotions. Soren's orders echoed in his head, a constant mantra that tugged at the edges of his conscience. The voice was a harsh reminder of what was at stake.

Amidst the weight of his infernal obligations, another voice, soft and forgiving, intertwined with his thoughts. Owlen's words, gentle and delicate, were floating through his mind. *Finn, my dear friend, you don't need to tread this dark path. There is still time to do the right thing.* A sudden surge of memories flooded his mind. Memories of the countless millennia he had spent alongside Owlen. The stolen moments of camaraderie, laughter, and even shared sorrow —an unbreakable bond.

Finn clenched his jaw, his fingers curling into tight fists. He knew that succumbing to Owlen's voice now would be a dangerous indulgence—a weakness he could not afford. This was the moment of truth; a pivotal crossroads where his loyalty to Hell and his history with Owlen collided head-on. He closed his eyes, trying to shut out the competing voices that waged war within him. The mortal's demise was non-negotiable, and failure was not an option this time. His own fate hung in the balance. Finn's eyes snapped open as he forcefully pushed Owlen's voice aside. This was no time to allow himself the luxury of such a gentle sound.

His fingers trembling slightly, Finn raised a hand and slowly swiped the air in front of the door. The green began to fade and swirl into an eerie haze, forming an invisible portal into the girl's private realm. For a moment he remained on the threshold, becoming a silent observer into her life. He could sense both innocence and tragedy within the dreary walls. A small table, modestly set for one, suggested that this mortal most likely leads a solitary life. This could potentially work in Finn's favor, since disrupting her life would have fewer complications.

A picture frame resting on top of a small mantel caught his attention. Although he couldn't make out their faces through the swirling fog, Finn could feel a sense of sorrow radiating from the photo, and a flicker of emotion stirred within him. His heart ached, inexplicably. Demons weren't meant to feel empathy, and he shook his head, reminding himself to focus on the assignment.

Finn's auburn hair shifted in the breeze as he tried to catch a glimpse of the rest of the room from beyond the haze. His eyes moved to a stack of cardboard boxes in the far corner—a telltale sign of recent upheaval. Perhaps belongings in transit from a move, or memories packed away, too difficult to face —a bitter reminder of human fragility. Finn's contemplative silence was interrupted by the sound of running water in the distance.

*She was here.*

He glanced behind him to ensure he was alone, and with determination hardening his features, Finn silently stepped through the doorway, the hazy energy closing behind him.

He quickly focused on the stack of boxes as infernal power surged within his hands. He summoned  flames which danced obediently on his fingertips. No longer hazy, the boxes would now play a vital role in this orchestrated chaos. The flames leapt hungrily from his fingertips, consuming the cardboard and the contents within. Fire spread quickly, devouring memories and filling the air with black, billowy smoke.

Smoke detectors wailed their warning, shattering the serenity of Scarlett's solitude. She jolted from her deep thoughts, her heart pounding in her chest as the piercing alarms echoed through her apartment. Droplets of water splashed onto the bathroom tile while she hastily dried her hands on her pants, faucet still running. As she raced toward the living room, a gasp escaped her throat. The heat hit her like a solid wall, causing her to instinctively shield her face.  Her eyes widened from under her arm at the sight before her—a blaze of fiery orange devouring her belongings, and in a blink, completely surrounding her.

"Help! Somebody please help me!" Scarlett's voice was raw with desperation as she cried out, her call barely audible over the crackling of the flames. She turned, desperately trying to find a way out, but the fire stretched to the ceiling, blocking every exit. Her eyes darted around the room, searching for any possible escape, but there was none. The realization struck her with a paralyzing sense of hopelessness. She screamed again. Her call for help echoed off the walls—a frantic plea unheard by anyone else but the demon who caused the destruction.

Smoke filled the room, thick and suffocating, stinging her eyes and clawing at her throat. She attempted to scream again, but all she could do was cough uncontrollably.

Finn watched from the smoky shadows, waiting for her demise and ready to collect her soul when the time was right. His heart was pounding as fiercely as the flames themselves.

*It was working.*

As the smoke began to take its toll, her fading breaths struck something deep within him. Sympathy, guilt—emotions he couldn't afford right now. Still concealed in the thick billows, he found himself torn between his demonic duty and an inexplicable force to act. His red eyes pierced through the smoke, locking onto her face, which held a final look of desperation. Their gazes met, and the shrill alarms and crackling of burning debris seemed to go silent in that moment.

Her figure, surrounded by the deadly tongues of fire, radiated an ethereal beauty that pierced through the darkness of his existence. A charged connection sent shock waves through his veins. A foreign sensation coursed through him —an emotion he had never known. Just as magnetic as his bond to Owlen, but inexplicably awakening a sense of longing and protectiveness. The connection to this mortal was unlike anything he had ever felt. Her desperate need for salvation awakened a part of him he had thought was lost to the darkness—a desire to guard her, to hold her, to take her from this place.

He loved her.

The decision was instantaneous. Her safety was now his priority. Finn charged forward through the smoke and flames. The heat seared around him, leaving his skin unharmed. With a surge of strength, he swept her up into his arms, his black wings unfurling and surrounding her like a protective cocoon. He caught a glimpse of her face through the haze and smoke, and the terror in her features had turned to confusion and disbelief. Their eyes locked once again, and in that moment, he knew his heart had shifted. Holding her tightly, Finn closed his eyes and focused on his destination. She wouldn't be safe here if Soren knew she was still alive. Finn thought of that delicate voice he tried so hard to push from his mind before the chaos he had caused. Leaving the inferno behind, Finn took her to the only place that came to mind—a  place he hadn't stepped foot on in a very long time.

Morvina's high heels clacked loudly against the unforgiving stone floor, announcing her arrival as she made her way to Soren's office. She looked very put-together in a black skirt that matched her clacking shoes. A badge with the title *Overseer of Infernal Assignments* was pinned to her red shirt. Her dark hair was slicked into a tight bun, which pulled her eyes back slightly, and her features were etched with a permanent expression as though she had just eaten something unbearably sour.

Pushing the door open without hesitation or invite, she entered the office and found Soren sitting on his smoldering throne. He looked down at her from beneath his dark cloak and raised an eyebrow. "Morvina, what are you doing here? Shouldn't you be meeting with your agents?"

"I have some... news," she announced, her voice a mixture of concern and unease. "About Finneas."

Soren leaned back, his fingers interlocked beneath his chin. "Ah, Finneas." A smirk stretched across his face, visible from where Morvina stood. "Has he been spotted by the mortal? Are we about to witness another one of his delightful failures?"

Not giving into his amusement, Morvina's gaze remained fixed on her boss. He sat up, clearing his throat, his smirk fading.

"Well," he said, "there will be some paperwork involved, but you know what to do, Morvina. Have an agent take care of the mortal. Deliver the soul to the Intake Office when they are finished. Also, summon Finneas for me. I'll be the one to issue his expulsion." He sat back in his throne, shooing his hand at her, dismissively.

Morvina's expression darkened, her sour lips pressed into a thin line. "It's worse, sir," she said. She took several slow steps closer. Her eyes bore into his as she crossed her arms.

*"Much worse."*

# CHAPTER THREE

## ANGEL

In the solitude of Luminara, Owlen often found himself in the gardens, surrounded by his creation. Despite Finn's absence, Owlen remained a faithful guardian of their shared world. He found a sense of purpose, an anchor that kept him grounded. His days were filled with meticulous puttering, and as he treated everything he touched with unwavering care, he held a silent hope that one day Finn would return to their paradise.

Owlen's gardens were a testament to his boundless creativity. Rows upon rows of carefully planted flowers melded together into a beautiful, mosaic masterpiece. He knew each flower intimately, nurturing their own needs and preferences. Kneeling down, fingers as gentle as whispers, he would coax each blossom to unfurl into its otherworldly beauty, welcoming it into his realm. These gardens were a tangible manifestation of the goodness that flowed through his very being, and the silent yearning that had settled in his heart.

Overhead, a beautiful display of avian wonders took to the skies. These exquisite birds, breeds unseen by any human, twirled and looped with effortless grace. As they descended from their flight, they found rest in the embrace of towering, winding trees. Their wings of amethyst, rose, and gold formed a kaleidoscope of color among the leaves like tiny jewels. Owlen would listen to their song resonating through the branches while the soft breeze touched his golden hair.

When the blanket of twinkling stars stretched across the night, he became a silent observer of the familiar cosmos above. The babbling stream provided a lullaby for the world around him, and his mind would often drift to Finn. He would wonder about his whereabouts, knowing Finn would forgo sleep to wander the shadows in secrecy. Owlen's heart ached with concern, imagining Finn among the demonic creatures of the night. He wondered what thoughts might occupy his friend's mind while the world was quiet and still.

The time between their meetings seemed like an eternity. When Finn was safe from the watchful eye of Soren, Owlen would travel to the mortal realm, seeking him out wherever he may be. His pull toward Finn was like a magnet, allowing Owlen to find him in any corner, any alley.

In the midst of their secret meetings, the two shared a love of traveling through the fabric of time. With a single glance, they would reach out to each other, joining hands. And then, as if guided by an invisible force, their surroundings would reshape before their eyes, taking them to the towering pyramids of ancient Egypt, or a hill overlooking a beautiful countryside, not yet touched by humankind.

As the moments ticked away, Finn would feel the tug of his demonic duties growing stronger. With a final lingering glance at the world around them, the two would part ways—each returning to their respective paths, waiting with anticipation until they could meet again.

Over the last century, their journeys had become more sporadic, as Finn's obligations trespassed on the precious time they once shared. Owlen's heart ached with a silent understanding of the struggle Finn was facing, knowing that his loyalties to the dark side were driving a wedge between them. Refusing to let Soren steal their cherished moments entirely, Owlen would find Finn whenever the opportunity allowed. With patience and persistence, he would often remind Finn of the goodness he saw in him, usually leading him out of whatever nefarious deed he had been tasked with that time. Owlen's unwavering belief in Finn became a lifeline that guided him through the complexities of this dark existence, a reminder of a life that was still within reach.

That afternoon's outing to meet Finn in the city led Owlen back to his small cottage that sat next to the gardens, in the heart of Luminara. The cozy, one-story structure blended seamlessly with the natural beauty surrounding it. The exterior, built from warm, honey-colored stone and wood, gave it an inviting and timeless appeal. Ivy gracefully climbed the walls, surrounding the cottage with a gentle hug. Round windows and patchwork shingles made it look like a fairy garden estate.

Inside, Owlen paced back and forth, his hands clasped tightly behind his back. The familiar surroundings of his living room—the worn, leather-bound books on their shelves, the comforting collection of trinkets—did nothing to ease his anxiety. The thought of his dearest friend involved in some important sinister matter with Soren gnawed at him in a way he couldn't explain.

He moved through the small, comfortable space, tidying the already pristine shelves, desperate to keep his mind occupied. His hands moved almost mechanically as his thoughts became consumed by Finn, and the possibility that he could slip deeper into darkness. He couldn't help but replay their recent conversation, knowing Finn had been hiding pain in his eyes.

He traced his fingers absentmindedly over the spines of his ancient books when a subtle shift caught his attention. The air around him had changed, charged with a familiar energy. His heart skipped a beat, and he stood still, straining to understand the sensation. It was a subtle yet profound awareness, a feeling that resonated deep within him.

Finn was nearby.

His heart began to quicken as he approached the cottage door, his shaking hand hesitating before swinging it open. To his astonishment, Finn stood in the doorway, cradling something in his arms that was as fragile as it was unexpected.

"Good Heavens!" Owlen breathed, his voice carrying a mix of shock and wonder. "Finn..is this..."

Finn glanced at Owlen, a rare hint of vulnerability flickered in his eyes. "Yeah," he replied, his voice uncharacteristically soft. "This is Scarlett... the *delicate* matter from earlier."

He set Scarlett down gently, his eyes fixed on her as she struggled to take in her new surroundings. Her breath came in quick, shallow gasps, her body trembling from the shock of the recent fire and the abrupt, bewildering change in her environment. She looked around, her wide eyes reflecting a mixture of confusion and awe. Her gaze lifted to meet Owlen's. "Hi," she said, offering him a shy smile.

Owlen extended a friendly smile, his features genuinely warm. "Hello, Scarlett. It's such a pleasure to meet you."

Finn's lips curled into a slight smirk. "This angel has been my best friend for..." he hesitated, shifting his eyes between Scarlett and Owlen. What he was about to say could certainly be overwhelming for a mortal. "For about 6000 years."

Finn and Owlen watched as Scarlett's brown eyes filled with confusion. A mix of surprise and disbelief flicked across her face. She blinked a few times, processing what she just heard. "Six... six thousand years? How is that even possible? How is *any* of this possible?"

Finn turned to Scarlett. He grabbed her face gently with his palms, his crimson eyes looking into hers with protective reassurance. "It's a very long story," he said. "One we'll gladly tell you tomorrow if you'll be willing to listen, but for now, all that matters is you're alive."

Scarlett's knees buckled slightly as she was looking into his eyes. She couldn't help but be mesmerized by this beautiful creature who entered her life so unexpectedly. She could feel an unspoken connection with him. Realizing she was staring, she blinked away quickly, her cheeks turning pink. "So... you're both angels, then?" she asked, clearing her throat.

"Not exactly, I..." Finn was about to explain, but was interrupted by Owlen's confusion.

"What do you mean *all that matters is that she's alive*? Why wouldn't she be alive?" He was beginning to question the events that could have led them there.

"My apartment was on fire," Scarlett offered, her eyes widening as she recalled the heroic tale. "I don't even know how he found me but luckily he was there. He saved me, just in time."

Owlen raised his eyebrows in surprise, his voice tinged with disbelief. "You *saved* her?"

Finn didn't answer. He pulled Scarlett into his chest in a warm embrace, his eyes locked onto Owlen's. A silent look of understanding was shared between them, and Owlen knew they would talk later. Owlen gestured toward the open doorway, ushering them inside with an inviting sweep of his arm. "Come in, then, my dear. You must need rest after such an ordeal."

Scarlett had been through a whirlwind of events, and her mind and body were both exhausted. The wooden floor creaked slightly underfoot as Owlen led the way through the cozy living space to the cottage's quaint bedroom. The soft glow of candlelight created a soothing ambiance, and the room seemed to welcome her with open arms.

"Here we are," Owlen announced with a tender smile, gesturing toward the inviting bed, each pillow perfectly placed on top of several fluffy blankets. "Rest now. You're safe here, and in the morning we will answer any questions you have."

"And you'll *both* be here?" she asked quietly, sleepiness taking over her eyes.

"Yes, we will both be here." The realization of Finn and this new friend staying with him brought a genuine sparkle to his eyes. His expression softened further as he placed a hand on her shoulder. "Sleep well," he whispered. Then, with a gentle wave of his hand, the candle blew out, and he left her to rest.

Soren tapped his leathery fingertips on the obsidian desktop, his dark eyes narrowing in frustration. Before him, Morvina, with her sour face, watched him with a critical eye. "He needs to be destroyed," she said impatiently. "This isn't just about failures, it's about the potential loss of valuable resources."

"Morvina, you know the revised code inside and out. We are not advised to destroy any demons until further notice—not even Finneas."

Morvina was seething, her normally fierce demeanor was amplified with frustration. "This is unacceptable. We still need to collect the mortal's soul, but Finneas has taken her to some kind of *celestial* plane. Our agents won't be able to reach her. We need to figure out a way to deal with this swiftly and mercilessly."

Soren's expression turned stoic. His thoughts were focused on a more intricate plan that had begun to take shape within his cunning mind. "Patience, Morvina," he responded, his voice carrying a cool reassurance. "There is a way to handle this situation that will prove *far* more rewarding than mere elimination."

Morvina's brows furrowed, her skepticism evident. "Explain."

Soren's gaze remained steady. His mind swirled with wicked thoughts as he laid out his plan. "Agents are bound by limitations, but *I* am not. I will go to their realm myself." Soren's eyes gleamed with malevolent intent. He envisioned himself stepping onto their protected land, tainting the purity of the surroundings. Descending upon the tranquil haven, bringing chaos to their serene paradise. With a sinister chuckle, Soren gleamed with satisfaction. "When all is said and done," he assured her, "Finneas will be nothing more than a broken shell of a demon—a reminder to anyone who dares to deceive me."

As Scarlett lay on the comfortable bed she was too exhausted to think of the day's events any longer. Her eyes grew heavy, and the room was darkening, pulling her into sleep, when a glimmer caught her attention. Her eyes fluttered open and she turned her gaze toward the large, round window. There, against the canvas of the dark sky, was Earth in spectacular radiance, with the Moon floating nearby. It was a sight beyond her wildest dreams, and now wide-awake, she stared in awe at its breathtaking majesty.

Her heart raced with a mix of wonder and unease. The sight of Earth, so far away and yet so captivatingly close, gave her a sense of homesickness and longing. She yearned for the familiar, to return to the ruins of her life and once again pick up the broken pieces. And while uncertainty still lingered, there was also an undeniable curiosity that ignited within her—a burning desire to see where the road with Finn would lead her.

Determined to get a better look at this magnificent sight, Scarlett quietly stepped out of bed and found the cottage's entrance. She stepped outside, the cool air brushing her skin, and found herself drawn to a cozy spot in the garden, next to the stream. Seated within the countless sleeping flowers, she gazed up at the sky, her mind a swirl of thoughts and emotions. She pondered the events that brought her to such a mysterious place. Looking up at the place that was once home, she was torn between the known and the unknown.

A breeze carried the voices of Finn and Owlen through the night air. She tilted her head slightly, secretly listening to their conversation. Owlen's voice held the gentle, yet probing tone, of a friend seeking answers. "Finn, I cannot help but think about that fire. Scarlett deserves to know the truth, don't you think? She placed her trust in us."

Finn responded with reluctant honesty. "And she will... in time. You know now what Soren ordered. Killing her wasn't an option when I saw her. I couldn't... I couldn't let her die." The weight of Finn's confession hung in the air, while he added words that sent a chill down Scarlett's spine. "She isn't safe there anymore. Once he finds out she's alive, he'll come for her. He won't rest until he has her soul. This is the only way."

Scarlett's heart raced as the realization dawned upon her. She had been right to question how she was rescued. How he found her so easily. Her fists tightened as her mind raced with a mixture of emotions—confusion, fear, anger. She hadn't asked to be thrown into this conflict and here she was, caught in the middle of truth and lies. Just as the weight of their words settled upon her, Scarlett's presence was acknowledged by a pair of gazes turning her way. Finn and Owlen were both looking at her, their eyes wide with aware-ness that she had been listening.

Caught in the moment, Scarlett's heart began to race. She found herself torn between wanting answers and wanting to go home, away from this place and its dark secrets. Sadness filled Owlen as he turned and quietly withdrew to the cottage, giving the two some needed privacy. His thoughts were racing with understandable concern for Scarlett, while also feeling the weight of Finn's hidden turmoil.

Outside, the air was heavy with emotion as Finn settled beside Scarlett. He adopted an uncharacteristic gentleness as he watched her, his usually sharp edges softened by unfamiliar tenderness. He was desperate to mend this brand new bond that had already been fractured.

Scarlett's eyes were full of unshed tears, while her face remained emotionless and numb. Her trembling words held accusation and stark realization. "So it was you. You started the fire... destroyed all my belongings, almost killing me. And then you brought me here like some kind of hero?"

Finn's response was delicate, as if Owlen was there, helping him with the words. "Yes, it was me. I started the fire and for that I am truly sorry." He leaned in slightly, his gaze locked onto hers. He needed her to see the depths of his sincerity, the layers of his internal struggle. "But there's more. A demon named Soren, a much greater demon, gave me the job of collecting your soul. I was supposed to kill you, but I couldn't."

Scarlett's tears fell freely now, her long, brown hair falling in disarray around her face. She shook her head slightly as she gazed up at Earth. It seemed much more distant now, her familiar life far out of reach. "So that's it?" she asked. "Everything's different now? I can't go back?"

Finn's eyes dropped, his gaze shadowed by regret. "You can't go back," he admitted. His heart ached with the truth of his words. Silence stretched between them. The vast garden was an unspoken observer of their shared uncertainty. Finn's crimson eyes held vulnerability and pain as he spoke again with a desperate plea in his shaky voice. "It was the only way to keep you safe, Scarlett. Please, believe me."

Scarlett's eyes snapped from him. Her features hardened as she took a deep breath and wiped her tears. "You set my entire life on fire. You ruined everything. I don't want to know you anymore. I hate you." Without casting a glance toward Finn, she rose silently and walked to the cottage, leaving him alone in the night.

Scarlett sat on the edge of the bed. The weight of the night's truth was too heavy for sleep to come. A soft knock on the door pulled her away from her thoughts. She looked up to see Owlen standing there. His expression was one of concern, but he carried himself with a polite and respectful air.

"May I come in?" he asked in a hushed tone. His voice was strangely comforting. Scarlett gave a slight nod and Owlen stepped into the room. He settled into a chair next to the bed, his eyes focused on her with empathy and understanding. "Scarlett, I can only imagine the pain you must be experiencing right now. Learning the truth about Finn and his actions must be overwhelming."

Scarlett's gaze shifted to her hands, her fingers tracing the delicate patterns on the bed sheet. She didn't speak, but the turmoil within her was evident in her expression. Owlen's eyes were kind as he understood her silence and continued.

"You're not alone in feeling this way. Finn's actions were certainly unexpected, even for me."

Scarlett wiped her eyes and looked at him, speaking with frustration in her voice. "But why? Why would he choose to set the fire?"

Owlen sighed. "I know it's difficult to understand why he would take orders to end the life of an innocent person. I, myself, have questioned his loyalties to Soren many times. But he defied him. That's so important for you to see. He literally *defied* Hell for you. He acted out of love."

Scarlett's face stung with dried tears as she tried to process everything. "But how do I know? How can I trust him? When he wrapped his arms around me, I thought... I don't know. Everything has been a lie so far."

Owlen looked at her with a reassuring smile. "I have the ability to see into a person's soul—the deepest thoughts of their mind. It's not just about what they do, but about their intentions, their true nature. I have always been able to see the goodness in Finn, despite the demon exterior. I can assure you, he acted out of true love for you."

Scarlett's eyes held a hint of hope. "And what do you see in my heart?" she asked, curiously.

Owlen's smile held a warm, knowing look as he met her eyes. "You love him too. Inexplicably, yes, but you love him. A love so deep and so sudden can certainly be confusing." Scarlett's breath caught in her throat, her heart suddenly bare before her.

"To be honest," Owlen continued, warmly, "I'm actually very grateful for you. I've always had a way of getting Finn out of certain... situations. But this time it was different. Nothing I said was going to change his mind. He said he had no choice, and that terrified me. Demons who are backed into corners are capable of horrible things." His voice was gentle but earnest. "Following orders, killing an innocent girl, that would have changed him. I could never bring him back from that. I couldn't bear to see him lost to that kind of darkness. But his love for you made him choose a different path... even if he is fumbling through it," he chuckled softly. "So for you, I will be eternally grateful."

The depth of Owlen's insight both startled and moved Scarlett. She began to realize that there may be more to Finn's actions than what she saw on the surface. It was a revelation that left her with a new understanding for the demon. Scarlett swallowed to keep her tears at bay. "Thank you, Owlen," she whispered. "For being honest with me...for caring."

Owlen stood up slowly, offering a warm smile. "Please give him a chance, my dear. I know you will see that he is genuine, and hopefully you will be able to forgive him." And with that, Owlen nodded respectfully and left her room, leaving Scarlett alone in her thoughts.

As the Moon and Earth cast their soft glow through the window, Scarlett's mind began to work on a plan. Something that would hopefully bridge the gap she created between herself and Finn. With a deep breath, she settled back onto her bed, her mind buzzing with thoughts of what lay ahead. *Tomorrow, I'll fix this*, she thought, and she knew just how she would do it.

# CHAPTER FOUR

## GOOD

The next morning arrived with soft, golden light filtering through the bedroom window. Scarlett's determination from the previous night only grew stronger, and she was ready to mend things with Finn. As she sat up, she found herself greeted by a delightful surprise. A tray filled with a mouthwatering assortment of breakfast treats was carefully arranged on her bed. A small folded card with beautiful calligraphy read: *A small gesture of friendship. Enjoy—Owlen.*

*Of course Owlen was behind this,* she thought, smiling. She savored every bite of the delectable breakfast, and as she sat on the edge of the bed to put on her sneakers, she realized she needed to use the bathroom. Embarrassment washed over her at the thought of having to ask where it might be.

She didn't remember seeing one as Owlen had shown her to the bedroom the night before. Unease crept in as she considered the fact that angels and demons wouldn't have use for a bathroom.

Realizing she couldn't afford to wait any longer, she took a deep breath and walked out of the bedroom to figure it out on her own. Perhaps a private spot outside. She was hoping not to run into Owlen or Finn on the way, and spare herself from having to discuss it with them. In the small hallway, she noticed something that made her stop in her tracks—a door next to the bedroom that hadn't been there the previous night. It stood slightly ajar, and she pushed it open, curiously. To her amazement, an exquisitely appointed bathroom was there, where a wall had previously been.

The toilet was a welcome sight, situated discreetly next to a small shower.  As she flushed, the water swirled and disappeared out of sight. She washed her hands at the beautiful porcelain sink, its basin adorned with delicate floral patterns. On the counter, there was an array of toiletries neatly arranged—lavender-scented soap, a small jar of face cream, a toothbrush, a tube of toothpaste, and a silver hairbrush, much fancier than any she had ever owned. The attention to detail was astonishing, and Scarlett couldn't help but smile. It was clear that Owlen had thought deeply about what a young woman might need to feel comfortable, even in such an unfamiliar place.

Scarlett noticed a neatly folded set of clothes on the edge of the shower—a pair of blue jeans and a purple t-shirt, identical to the ones she was wearing, with undergarments tucked discreetly inside. She quickly undressed, peeling off the sooty clothes that clung to her skin. As the warm water rushed over her, she sighed in relief, feeling the grime and sweat from yesterday's ordeal wash away.

After getting dressed, she picked up the hairbrush and began to brush her long, damp hair into place. As she did so, she caught sight of herself in the round, ornate mirror above the sink, and for a moment, she saw her mother's eyes in her own reflection. Despite the warmth and charm of the bathroom, the familiarity of seeing her mother looking back at her gave Scarlett a pang of homesickness.

Her reflection seemed out of place in this otherworldly setting. It was as if she was on a vacation from which she could never return. The comforting feeling of coming home after a long trip, setting down her suitcase, and sinking into her own bed was something that would never come. She needed to come to terms with the fact that, because of recent events, this strange and magical place would be her home now. This situation was hard for everyone involved, and she resolved to find a way to adapt.

As she stepped outside, her eyes widened at the breathtaking beauty that surrounded her. Fragrant blooms in colors she had never seen painted the countryside surrounding the cottage. A stream meandered its way through the immense garden like a silver ribbon, its waters glistening in the sunlight while dancing over smooth stones and pebbles. The air was alive with the hum of insects—the buzz of bees and the fluttering of butterflies as they flitted from bloom to bloom. Scarlett gasped as she caught sight of Earth, hanging in splendor, its beautiful blues and greens, peeking just over the horizon.

Every step she took awakened new sights and smells. Standing in the middle of this oasis, Scarlett felt a sense of gratitude wash over her. She was thankful to be welcome in such a beautiful world. She spotted Owlen carefully tending to the very flowers that surrounded her. His hands were gently gliding over the blooms that appeared to awaken with his touch. He was whispering something as each beautiful petal slowly unfurled in his palm. The daylight danced across his face accentuating his kind eyes and gentle smile. As Scarlett walked over to him, her fingertips brushed the tops of the velvety flowers.

"Good morning, Owlen," she said as he stood up to welcome her. "Thank you so much for breakfast. It was delicious. It looked almost too perfect to eat. And the bathroom, the clothes... really, I can't thank you enough."

Owlen chuckled warmly. "It's my pleasure. Honestly, It's so nice to have someone here to create meals for." He leaned in, lowering his voice. "If there is anything missing in the bathroom that you may need, please let me know."

"Thanks so much. You've made this whole situation a little easier for me. I really appreciate you," she said. Owlen blushed slightly, looking down at the blooms that were hugging his legs.

"I had no idea how beautiful this place is," Scarlett said, still looking around in amazement. "I've never seen anything like it."

Owlen's smile widened with pride. "I'm so glad you like it. Creating Luminara truly has been a labor of love. Even Finn seemed impressed. He said, *You really outdid yourself, angel.* That is definitely a compliment, coming from him."

"Where is Finn, by the way?" Scarlett asked. She was thankful that Owlen mentioned him, although she couldn't settle the sudden knots in her stomach at the sound of his name.

Owlen's expression fell a bit as he looked toward the other side of the cottage. "He's been in the same spot all night. He isn't feeling his best, as you can imagine. I can sense that he's dealing with his own thoughts right now, and regretting hurting you so much."

Scarlett's heart ached at the thought of Finn in so much turmoil. She turned back to Owlen. "Thank you," she said, sincerely. "For everything you've done and for our talk last night. It means a lot to me."

"You're very welcome," he said warmly, touching her shoulder. "I'm here if you need anything."

With a grateful smile, Scarlett excused herself and began to make her way to the spot where she had left Finn last night. The events of the previous day had left her with a whirlwind of unfinished emotions, and she was determined to face them head-on.

Her breath quickened with every step she took toward him. She rubbed her damp palms against her jeans in an attempt to dry them. A subtle tremor moved through her fingers, and she clenched her fists to hide it, as her heart pounded so loudly she feared he might hear it.

As Scarlett walked closer, she noticed Finn sitting beneath a sprawling tree, his gaze fixed on the ground. His expression seemed solemn, and the weight of their complicated situation still hung in the air. She swallowed hard and tucked a stray lock of hair behind her ear, trying to muster the courage for what she was about to do. She took a deep breath and prepared herself for a conversation that could potentially shape their future. She settled down next to Finn, the soft grass beneath them providing a hint of comfort. The space between them was charged with unspoken words, and for a while, they both sat in silence.

It was Finn who finally spoke first, his voice gentle as he inquired, "Did you sleep well?"

Scarlett glanced at him, noticing the vulnerability in his eyes that he tried to conceal. "Not really," she admitted with a small, understanding smile. "My mind was racing, you know?"

Finn nodded, his gaze still averted. He found it difficult to meet her eyes, his heart heavy with knowledge of the pain he had caused. He feared her rejection and the thought that she might understandably want him to take her from this place and never see him again. So he kept his gaze fixed on the grass, allowing the tension between them to settle.

"Owlen came to talk to me last night," Scarlett said softly, shifting her focus on the horizon. "He explained everything."

Finn's head turned slightly with interest. "He did?"

Her gaze shifted to Owlen who was feeding some birds from his palm nearby. There was a fondness in her voice as she continued. "Yes. He really helped me see things differently. I'm so glad he's here."

A mix of relief and gratitude flooded through Finn at her words. He couldn't help but steal a fleeting glance at Owlen, a silent expression of appreciation for his friend's intervention. "Yeah, he has a way of shedding light on things."

Scarlett turned her attention back to Finn, her gaze meeting his profile. Her heart ached at the pain and uncertainty in his eyes. With a gentle, reassuring smile, she spoke again. "I want you to know that I don't hate you. There's a lot I *don't* know, but I know I'm safe with you now. Despite everything, it means a lot to me that you chose to save my life."

Finn's breath caught in his throat as he finally turned to look at her, his eyes meeting hers. The weight that had been resting on his shoulders lightened as he realized she wasn't entirely pushing him away like he had feared. "You don't have to trust me right away," he said, his voice soft but hopeful. "I just... I need you to know that I'm so sorry for starting the fire. I can't take it back, and I'll never forgive myself for that. I just couldn't bear the thought of being the one to take your life."

Scarlett's heart swelled at the raw honesty he allowed himself to show. She reached out, placing her hand on his in the grass. "I know. I believe you," she said softly, her eyes locked onto his. Her touch was gentle and comforting. For a brief moment they simply gazed at each other, their unspoken feelings hanging in the air like a delicate thread. The tension that once divided them was now replaced with a growing sense of understanding and connection.

"Thank you," Finn whispered, his voice barely audible, his crimson eyes never leaving hers. A weight had been lifted from his heart, and in that moment he allowed himself to believe in the possibility of redemption, and a future that held more than just darkness.

Scarlett turned to fully face him, her eyes following her fingers as they reached for him, and gently traced his cheek, leaving a trail of warmth on his skin. Finn's breath hitched as her touch sent a shiver down his spine. Her heart raced as she gently ran her hand through Finn's hair, feeling the soft, auburn strands slip through her fingers.

Her eyes locked onto his, searching for any sign of hesitation, but all she saw was mirrored intensity. Slowly, she leaned in, her lips trembling slightly with a mix of nervousness and excitement. Finn's warm breath brushed against her face, creating a wave of goosebumps across her skin. Scarlett leaned forward, her lips meeting his. A spark ignited between them, sending a rush of warmth throughout their bodies. Her hand tightened in his hair, anchoring herself in the moment. The kiss was a combination of all the emotions that had been building between them. A lingering kiss of understanding, forgiveness, and an unspoken commitment.

Finn's heart pounded in his chest as he responded to the kiss, his fingers gently finding their place against the small of her back, pulling her closer. His lips moved against hers with a tenderness he had never known. As the kiss deepened, Finn knew without a doubt that he would give up Heaven and Hell a thousand times over just to stay in this moment—to savor the taste of her lips, the warmth of her touch, and the intoxicating sensation of truly being alive.

As they finally pulled away—their breaths mingling in the air—his eyes remained on hers. The kiss was a turning point for both of them, mending the fractures of their broken hearts with a love that, for Finn, was truly eternal. As he looked at Scarlett, his heart beat with a purpose and determination to protect her at all costs. From that moment, he was no longer just a demon navigating the complexities of his existence; he was completely hers, willing to risk everything to keep her safe.

The sun climbed higher in the sky, its gentle rays danced through the leaves above, casting dappled patterns of light over Finn and Scarlett. They remained nestled in each other's arms, their conversation flowing as naturally as the stream beside them. Scarlett's laughter filled the air as she recounted stories from her childhood, while Finn listened with careful attention. His crimson eyes were locked on her as he hung on every word.

"So, *Letti Spaghetti* was your name, huh?" Finn chuckled playfully as he read the silver bracelet that hung from her delicate wrist.

"Well, it was a nickname, and it had nothing to do with food, thank you very much," she giggled. She was silent for a moment, then her smile faded slightly. Finn saw a brief glint of sadness in her eyes as she wrapped her hand around her wrist, concealing the bracelet.

"What is it?" he asked, placing his hand on hers.

"I was just wondering something," she said quietly, glancing up at the Earth in the distance. Finn's eyes glanced up as well, and he instantly understood her sadness.

"You're wondering about home," he said with a solemn tone.

"It's been a whole day now since the fire. Do you think anyone is looking for me?"

Finn squeezed her hand and looked down at his feet. He didn't know how to answer the delicate question of Scarlett's demise. She was missing or presumed dead. Neither one would help matters at this moment. Scarlett glanced at him and understood his silence. "I was just curious," she said with a half-smile. "I'm home now, with you."

Finn raised his crimson eyes to meet hers. "Thank you," he whispered. "I know it's been hard for you."

"Let's change the subject," Scarlett said, trying to lighten the mood. I want to hear about all the trouble you got into as a demon, *before* me, I mean." She looked at him with a playful smile.

Their voices could be heard throughout the garden as Finn found himself sharing stories from his own long existence. Tales of escaping his demonic duties, and shenanigans that left even him amused. Scarlett's eyes widened with wonder as he described one of his many failures that led him to her. "It was called the *Emerald Run*. Some kind of prestigious horse race back in 1901. You may have heard of it. My job was to cause an *accident* during the final stretch of the race—a sinkhole..." His voice deepened to add a dramatic effect to his tale. "...causing twenty horses and their riders to plummet to their deaths in front of hundreds of spectators."

Scarlett's mouth let out a slight gasp, and she sat up, eager to hear more. "So what happened? Did you do it?"

"*Me?*" Finn questioned, pointing to himself. "You really think *I'd* kill twenty horses? Or their riders, I suppose." He chuckled. "No. I couldn't do it. Instead I created a *distraction*. A fire in the horse stable before the race even started. All the riders and their families were forced to evacuate, leaving the horses behind in their locked stalls."

"What happened to the horses, then?" Scarlett asked, looking concerned.

"Can't be too sure. They never found the bodies," he answered with a smug smile. "But I *may* have seen roughly twenty crows flying from the burning building to safety, just in the nick of time."

Scarlett grinned at him. "I knew you weren't a monster," she said, nudging his shoulder.

"For years, every time I saw a group of crows, I half-expected them to start galloping," he smirked. "Definitely worth the trouble."

As they laughed, Owlen watched them from a distance like a faithful guardian. His heart swelled with happiness at the sight of Finn opening up, revealing a side of himself that had been buried for so long. This was the Finn he had always known. The one who could find joy in the simplest moments. The one who deserved happiness just as much as anyone.

In the midst of their conversation and laughter, Finn's gaze met Owlen's, and a silent understanding passed between them. Owlen was filled with contentment as he realized that his efforts, his creation of their home, had led to this very moment. Scarlett had found her place among them. Her presence was a blessing for Owlen. His blue eyes glistened as he took in the sight of Finn, who had once been consumed by darkness and isolation, now basking in the warmth of companionship once again.

As days unfolded into weeks, a sense of harmony and familiarity settled over the cottage they all shared together. The rhythm of their lives seemed to flow effortlessly. Owlen's gentle presence became a source of comfort for Scarlett. He would create exquisite meals and sit with her as she dined in a place he created just for her—a beautifully crafted wooden picnic table surrounded by thousands of purple flowers.

Between their meals together, Owlen guided her through the celestial garden, teaching her about the flowers and their unique properties. "You see," he'd explain, "these blooms are more than mere decorations. They are woven into the very fabric of our world—part of a delicate balance that sustains it. Every flower has its place here." Scarlett was filled with admiration for Owlen and all that he had to share. She felt as though she had known him for a lifetime.

The relationship between Scarlett and Finn had deepened as well. They spent their nights lying beneath the stars sharing stories, and quiet moments of connection that came with new love. Finn would hold Scarlett as she drifted to sleep, his gaze lingering on her peaceful smile. He felt a profound sense of gratitude for her presence in his life as he carefully watched her dream.

In the glow of the starlight, Finn's eyes would trace the delicate curve of her features, her every breath a reminder of the life he chose to protect. The weight of his own past seemed insignificant as he realized that this love is what truly mattered to him. He had once been a creator of chaos, serving Hell's intentions. Now he had found purpose in safeguarding this mortal's life. The three of them were a family. A constellation of hearts woven together by threads that defied separation.

The morning sun had just begun to cast its gentle rays over the tranquil landscape, painting everything in shades of gold. Scarlett stirred in Finn's arms, feeling the warmth of his embrace as a soft smile crossed her lips. The world around them was alive, as birds and flowers woke from their slumber.

However, a rumbling sound echoed from the horizon. A sound so foreign that it instantly caught their attention. Thunder, deep and ominous, rolled through the air, casting unease over their haven. As the distant rumbling drew nearer, Owlen emerged from the cottage, his usually warm smile replaced by a look of concern. He joined Finn and Scarlett in the garden, his gaze fixed on an approaching spectacle. A wall of dark clouds loomed on the horizon—an advancing mass that seemed to swallow everything in its path.

# CHAPTER FIVE

## EVIL

Scarlett's worry deepened as her eyes shifted between Finn and Owlen. "What's happening?" she asked. But they both appeared equally puzzled and alarmed. Seeking reassurance, she looked up at Finn who held her tighter, guarding her from whatever might be coming. Owlen on the other hand, stepped forward, his brow furrowed in concentration.

With a determined expression, Owlen extended his hand and gestured in a fluid motion, summoning his celestial powers to create a protective barrier. His intention was clear—to shield his dear friends from the impending unknown that was coming closer. However, as the wall of clouds neared, it became evident that his considerable abilities were being challenged by whatever unnatural force approached.

The tension in the air was undeniable. Fear coated every bit of Scarlett, and her fingers instinctively intertwined with Finn's. His grip offered a measure of comfort. It was a silent promise that he would do whatever it took to keep her safe.

The sky above continued to darken. The clouds in the distance were swirling with an eerie intensity that defied the nature of their peaceful world. The barrier Owlen had created wavered under pressure, its protective aura flickered out like a candle flame in the wind. Despite his efforts, the force drawing nearer was beyond anything he had ever encountered.

"Get back! Let me try!" Finn surged forward, placing himself between Scarlett, Owlen, and the encroaching darkness. His auburn hair ruffled in the harsh wind as he extended his hand, trying to summon his own protective magic against the looming force. Owlen held Scarlett tightly, unfurling his ivory wings to form an instinctive shield around them both, as Finn's efforts intensified.

But just as Finn was about to conjure his own defense, the ground beneath their feet quivered, causing them all to exchange alarmed glances. Then, with a violent tremor, the land split. The fracture quickly spread from the horizon to their feet. Wide-eyed, the three watched in shock as the crevice widened, exposing boiling lava in the depths below, bathing their faces in ghostly light. Rocks tumbled into the abyss as the land continued to tear apart. The radiant blooms of Owlen's beloved garden bowed in agony while being subjected to this newfound chaos.

As rolling storm clouds churned above the destroyed paradise, a sinister figure materialized in the sky. Soren descended with a haunting grace, his form shrouded in a dark billowing cloak that absorbed the light around him. Beneath the concealing folds of his cloak, Soren's most distinguishing feature came to light. A set of massive, bat-like wings unfurled in a frightening display of power, their tattered appearance clearly implying a history of torment and violence.

Soren's face, covered in burns and scars, bore a menacing smile that stretched across his leathery skin. His presence sent shivers through them all. As Scarlett clung tightly to Finn, Owlen attempted to shield her from view, but with a mere nod from Soren, he was flung backward with a violent force. He slammed against the cottage door and crumbled to the ground, his body completely frozen by dark magic. He was now a helpless spectator to the unfolding nightmare.

Finn's anger flared as he confronted Soren. "What in the Hell are you doing here?" he snarled, his red eyes ablaze with fury.

The wicked smile didn't leave Soren's face in the midst of Finn's threatening tone. "I believe we had an agreement, Finneas," he hissed. "You promised me a soul, so I'm here to collect."

Finn's eyes narrowed. "You're not touching her!" he spat. He clenched Scarlett tightly against his chest. He would take them both somewhere else to buy time, just like he pulled her out of the fire. But Soren was one step ahead of him. Before Finn could think of their escape, Soren's outstretched hand acted as a sinister vice, snatching Scarlett from Finn's grasp, pulling her toward him with a sinister strength. She now dangled from his hand by the neck over the bubbling, molten lava below. Her eyes were wide with terror as she began to struggle for air.

Finn's heart was pounding as he put up his hands in a gesture of surrender, sinking to his knees. His voice was loaded with desperation. "Please," he begged, his eyes locked on Scarlett. "Put her down safely. You can take me instead. This is all to punish me, right? Take me."

Soren's annoyance was evident, although his smile remained. Watching Finn beg had made the last eternal weeks of waiting completely worthwhile. "Finneas," he scoffed, "You should know better. We're advised not to destroy our fellow demons... for now. Also, you're forgetting that you're no longer welcome in Hell. To me, you're nothing more than a *disappointment*."

As Soren spoke, Finn's mind raced through desperate scenarios, and a determined plan took shape. He knew it was a perilous gamble, but if Soren dropped Scarlett, he was prepared to jump into action. He could summon his wings in an instant and catch her, taking her to safety.

Soren continued to dangle Scarlett carelessly over the glowing abyss, her struggles for breath growing more and more desperate. As her hands clutched at Soren's tight grasp, her silver bracelet broke from her wrist and fell to the glowing river below.

"Say your goodbyes, girl," Soren said to her. He pulled her close to his ear, mocking her mercilessly. "You'll have to speak louder, dear. I can't hear you." He gave a maniacal laugh and tightened his grip around her throat. Her fingernails frantically wrenched at Soren's hand, searching for any weakness.

Finn's desperation reached a fever pitch as he watched Scarlett struggle for breath, her face contorted in agony. His voice broke as he pleaded with Soren, tears mixing with rain that had begun to fall from the dark clouds overhead. "What do you want? Name it!" Finn cried out, his heart breaking at Scarlett's suffering. "Just give her back to me, please. I'll do anything you want... just give her back to me and let Owlen go." Owlen, frozen and powerless, could only watch in terror as the tense standoff between demon and demon unfolded.

Soren's grin widened at Finn's desperation. "*Anything*, you say? Interesting." He delighted in the power he held over the weakened demon. He savored Finn's plea for a moment before revealing his sinister request. "I'm feeling generous, so I'll make a little trade with you. You can have your friends, and I'll take your *wings*."

Finn's eyes widened in disbelief, and he felt a surge of anger and suspicion. "I don't understand. What use could you possibly have for my wings?"

Soren chuckled darkly. "Don't worry about my use for them, Finneas. That will come in time. But, If you don't want to give your friends their freedom, that's perfectly fine." He gripped Scarlett's throat even tighter. Her gasps became more desperate as her vision blurred.

Tears streamed down his face. Finn had no choice. He would protect her at all costs. "Take them," he said through clenched teeth. "Just let them go." Finn's voice quivered as he agreed to Soren's terms. A heavy weight settled in his chest, and he exchanged a desperate look with Scarlett. He wished he could reassure her, tell her everything would be alright. But the reality of their situation was squeezing his heart like Soren's grip.

Scarlett, her strength fading, mouthed the word "Don't," but the deal was done.

Finn's heart was pounding. With a heavy sigh, he closed his eyes and his black wings unfurled over him as he knelt to the ground. The embers on each feather still glowed through the beating rain. The wings that had been a part of him through light and dark, were now exposed and vulnerable.

Soren, watching Finn with a menacing smile, gestured downward with his other hand. In an instant, Finn's wings were brutally torn from his back and into Soren's fist. The force sent a shockwave of excruciating pain through him. A scream of anguish tore from Finn's throat. His fingers clawed at the ground as he was consumed by the searing torment. He writhed and convulsed, his mutilated and bloody back now visible through his ripped clothes. Each second was an eternity, a merciless reminder of the price he was willing to pay to save the ones he loved.

Scarlett's heart shattered with every scream that tore from Finn's lips. As she was near unconsciousness, she could only manage to reach a weak hand toward him. Tears fell down Owlen's cheeks freely as he witnessed the torment that his dearest friend endured. Searing pain filled his own chest, and in that moment he wanted more than anything to intervene and take his place.

Finn remained on his knees, blood spilling from his back onto the ground below. His voice trembled as he finally spoke. "Now... give her to me and let him go." Every word was an effort. Every breath, a struggle.

Soren, his eyes glistening at the sight of the fallen demon, released his hold on Scarlett and tossed her to the ground next to Finn, her neck covered in deep marks from his tight grip. Owlen was freed from his frozen state, and rushed to Scarlett's side to help her stand.

With one final, chilling laugh, Soren closed his fist and Finn's wings were obliterated instantly. Scarlett and Owlen watched, their hearts heavy, as feathers scattered into the stormy air like ashes. Their world seemed to mourn the loss of such beauty as the wind carried them down into the boiling depths.

Soren concluded his bargain. He achieved what he came for, at least for now. Laughter echoed through the chaotic storm clouds as he dematerialized into their ominous midst. As the wind calmed, and the skies cleared, the imminent danger was gone, but remnants of Soren's rampage still loomed on the horizon.

Owlen's eyes were filled with tears, but he couldn't afford to cry now. His friend needed help. Scarlett kneeled down and put her arm around her wounded demon. "Owlen, we have to get him inside."

With a collective effort they gently lifted Finn from the ground, and carefully helped him into the cottage. As they walked inside, Finn's steps were feeble and unsteady, his body aching and weakened. Owlen's gentle guidance was a steadying presence at his side, and Scarlett followed. Her stomach churned as she saw what remained of his mutilated back.

The journey was slow, and each step was filled with their silent promise to give him the comfort and care he desperately needed. With tender movements, Scarlett and Owlen guided Finn onto the bed, his form settling onto the mattress with a heavy sigh. His back exposed to them both, Scarlett's tear-filled eyes traced the lines of his wounds, her heart aching at the pain he endured because of her.

Owlen's gentle hands cleaned the torn remnants of Finn's back. He applied soothing balms made from his own celestial magic. His angelic touch could bring comfort and relief, but even his divine abilities had limits when faced with the aftermath of dark magic. He did everything he could to sooth his pain and make him as comfortable as possible. His presence was always a source of comfort, especially now. A reminder that Finn and Scarlett were not left to pick up the pieces alone.

Finn couldn't sleep—he could only lie in agony, waiting for relief to come. Scarlett's concern for her demon was evident in her eyes. As he stirred, she whispered to Owlen, desperate for answers. "Can't you use your powers to heal him? To grow his wings back? I've seen you do amazing things."

Owlen sighed, his expression reflecting the deep regret he felt. "My dear, I wish it were that simple. I would help him in an instant," he said quietly, his voice heavy with sorrow. "I have many powers as an angel, but there are certain things even I can't undo. The kind of dark magic Soren possesses is beyond my abilities to repair." He could see the disappointment in Scarlett's expression as he continued.

"Only another demon could undo what's been done here. But that, I'm afraid, is an impossibility. No demon would risk defying Soren to help our friend." He placed a hand gently on Finn's shoulder. "The consequences would be dire, as you could imagine." Owlen's eyes were brimming with tears as he confessed his regrets to Scarlett. "I wish now more than anything I had chosen the same path as Finn. If I had become a demon, myself, I could help him now in his time of need. Give him back what was taken from him."

Scarlett and Owlen finally emerged from the cottage after days of bedside care. Finn was resting more comfortably, so they ventured into the once-vibrant garden, now scarred by the terrible events. Owlen looked around with a deep sigh, taking in the damage from Soren's wrath. "Oh, my poor flowers," he said with sorrow. "They must have been so frightened through all of this."

The garden, once overflowing with celestial beauty, now showed visible scars of the recent chaos. A deep crevice still remained where the ground had split open, but the remnants of the boiling river within were now gone. The flowers that once surrounded their cozy cottage had mostly withered away. Yet, despite the destruction, there was still a promise of renewal in the air. Birds had returned to the bare branches of the trees, singing happily in the afternoon sun.

Scarlett's eyes were heavy with guilt as she took in the damage. "I'm so sorry, Owlen," she whispered, her voice trembling. "None of this would have happened if it weren't for me."

Owlen immediately moved to reassure her. "My dear friend," he said kindly, taking her hands into his, "please don't put any blame on yourself for Soren's actions. I've seen into Finn's heart through all of this. He would sacrifice his wings over and over again if it meant saving you, despite the pain he felt. He has no regrets for that sacrifice, and I have no regrets for mine."

"At least Soren's gone for good now," she said, looking toward the horizon, trying to be positive in their dismal surroundings.

Owlen's eyes, however, held a different emotion. He gazed at the distant storm clouds that still lingered, his expression troubled. Why were they still there? He chose not to worry Scarlett at that moment, so he offered a nervous smile instead. "Let's go check on our friend, and then I'll make you some dinner."

As they walked toward the cottage, they heard a stirring within. Finn was out of bed. He opened the door as they approached, and he was met with their smiling faces. Their joy at seeing him up and walking again warmed his heart. As Finn joined them outside, he moved with more ease than before, a sign that his recovery was well underway.

His back had improved thanks to Owlen's careful attention. He couldn't help but feel gratitude toward them both. With a heartfelt expression, Finn turned to his friends. "Thank you, both of you, for helping me through this."

"No need to thank us," Owlen said warmly. "We're a family. We're here for you, always." Scarlett nodded in agreement, gently wrapping her arms around his waist, well below his scars. Finn reached down gently and kissed her forehead. As the trio stood together, a distant rumble of thunder reached their ears. Finn and Owlen exchanged a look of concern, and the weight of what they knew was evident in their eyes.

Scarlett couldn't ignore the unease that they were both trying to hide. "I can see something is wrong," she said, looking between the two of them. "Please tell me what's happening."

Finn exchanged another worried look with Owlen before taking a deep breath. "He's coming back."

# CHAPTER SIX

## DEATH

The revelation of Finn's words struck Scarlett like a frigid wind. Her eyes widened in fear as her mind raced at the thought of what this meant. Her face drained of color—her breaths coming in shallow anxious bursts, and her friends' demeanor didn't help calm her.

Finn's panic manifested in restless movement, his footsteps echoing in the garden as he paced back and forth. He understood the grim reality all too well. His wings had been sacrificed to save Scarlett once, but now they were gone. He was utterly useless against Soren. His usual suaveness was thrown aside in the face of their situation.

"Soren... he's got a plan, and it's much worse than I imagined," he said to Scarlett, still pacing.

Scarlett looked at him, terror growing in her eyes. "What's he planning?"

Finn stopped in his tracks. He spoke as the realization was hitting him. "He wants to make sure I can't save you. Without my wings I won't be able to reach you if he decides to... *drop you*. This was his plan the whole time. He could easily just take your soul—nobody could stop him, but he wants to hurt me while doing it." He couldn't help but feel they were trapped in a merciless game, where the score was taken long before they had a chance to play.

Each word felt like a heavy stone, shattering any kind of hope Scarlett had of returning to normalcy. Her mind raced with a thousand thoughts, and a growing sense of helplessness washed over her. A lump formed in her throat, making it difficult to swallow, let alone speak. "Can't we just... run away? Hide somewhere? There must be someplace where he can't find us."

Finn's face darkened as he explained. "There isn't a corner of the universe where he can't find us. He's relentless. He won't stop chasing you."

Owlen was quietly weighing the gravity of the situation. His heart was heavy with the knowledge of what his friends would endure when Soren returned, and he was acutely aware that time was running out. He looked up and his gaze met Scarlett's, who was eagerly waiting for him to speak—to provide some sort of comfort like he always had. He always seemed to know the right course of action to take, and this time was no different. As tensions rose, Owlen locked eyes with Finn and finally spoke. "Finn, you know we only have one option. We..."

But with an instinctual understanding of what Owlen was hinting at, Finn shut him down with a raised hand before he could finish. "No. That's *not* an option."

Scarlett, unable to bear the weight of the unknown, felt her heart pounding as she waited for them to explain. What was this plan that could save her, and why was Finn adamantly refusing to consider it?

Owlen tried to reason with Finn, his voice full of desperation. "Finn, you *know* this is the only way. This would end it —all of it. We have to try."

Finn's frustration grew, and he raised his voice, shouting at Owlen. "No! I'm not doing that. Don't you understand? I *can't* do that." His helplessness was evident as he slumped onto the broken remnants of the wooden picnic table, burying his face in his hands. He gripped his hair tightly as if he could rip this unbearable choice away. Even as they argued, both Owlen and Finn knew deep down that this may be their only hope.

Scarlett, on the edge of her seat, her face pale with anxiety, couldn't face the uncertainty any longer. She pleaded with them, her voice trembling as she urged for answers. "Will someone please just tell me what's going on?"

Finn remained hunched over, his hands entangled in his auburn hair, unable to look her in the eyes. He let out a defeated yell—a scream of anguish that made her jump.

Turning to Owlen, Scarlett begged him with tear-filled eyes. "Why won't he talk to me? Please, Owlen, tell me the truth."

Owlen knew there was no way to avoid it any longer. He couldn't shield her from the truth, and time was running out. The growing thunder in the distance made that clear. He looked her in the eyes and spoke, choosing his words carefully. "The only way to make this stop—to make *Soren* stop—is for Finn to change you. To make you a demon."

Scarlett was silent for a moment as she processed what she just heard. "Is that even possible?" she inquired.

Owlen took a deep breath, his voice soft and reassuring. "Finn has never tried this before, but it's within his powers."

A mix of emotions crossed Scarlett's face—fear, uncertainty, and then surprisingly, a glimmer of hope. Her voice, although trembling, held a touch of optimism. "I can be immortal then? With Finn... with you?" She couldn't help but find a silver lining in the midst of despair. But as Scarlett ran to Finn, eager to embrace the idea of immortality together, to get on with this plan that was their last hope, he remained shut down. Something weighed heavy on his heart. More truths that were being hidden from her. She turned to Owlen once more, pressing him for answers. "What's wrong with him? Why doesn't he want this?"

Owlen approached her solemnly, taking her by the hand and leading her a few steps away from Finn, who was lost in his own troubled thoughts. He looked at her with kind, under-standing eyes, his voice hushed to keep their conversation private. "There's something about the idea of transformation that's deeply upsetting for Finn. You see, in order to change you, he would have to first remove your soul... essentially ending your life."

Owlen's gentle words hit her like a fist. Her eyes drifted off, out of focus, and she was unable to speak. *Be killed* or *be killed*. Her heart sank at the thought of her options.

Owlen understood her silence and continued, quietly. "You can see, then, why this is so difficult for our friend. He has sacrificed so much already to save you, to keep you safe... only to be the one who must ultimately end your life. It's a cruel choice, and it's the most painful thing he will ever face, even if it's for a greater purpose."

Once again Owlen had shed light on things. Her demon was facing an impossible choice. After a moment of reflection, Scarlett walked over to Finn and knelt down in front of him, gently lifting his face with her hands. As she looked into his eyes, she saw the torment that was consuming him, his expression drained of all hope. Scarlett finally found her voice. Her tone was filled with compassion and understanding as she tried to reassure him. "I trust you, *completely*. I know you can do this."

Tears welled in Finn's eyes as he voiced his doubts. "No, you don't understand—I can't. What if it doesn't work? If you don't... wake up, I'll never forgive myself. I'll have to live forever knowing what I did. I can't do it."

Scarlett's gaze remained steady as she held him. Her face was pale, but resolute. Now was not the time to waver. "Don't I get a say? Look, if I'm going to die anyway, at least let it be out of kindness and not some cruel, sadistic game. I can't bear the thought of him doing it. *Please.*"

Her plea sliced through Finn like a blade. His heart clenched as the weight of their only option pressed down on him. He had only ever heard stories of demons changing humans, but he had never seen it for himself, and the risks were immense. Failing meant losing her forever, but so did doing nothing. He couldn't deny her the only chance she had at living—even if it meant dying. And with that, Finn pulled her close, their tears mingling as they embraced. This was an impossible choice but they had made the choice together.

Owlen watched them, giving them a last fleeting moment of solace. But as the distant clouds were rolling closer, he knew time was slipping away. With a heavy heart, he approached them and gently placed a hand on Finn's shoulder. "It's time, my friends. We have to do this now."

Finn rose from the table and walked away, giving himself a moment to mentally prepare for what he was about to do. Scarlett's voice, soft and determined, reached his ears as she spoke to Owlen, seeking guidance on what to expect. "So how does this work? What do I have to do?"

Owlen took a deep breath and tried to control the sorrow in his voice as he explained the process. "You'll lie down, and Finn will lean over you. He will begin taking deep breaths from your mouth, drawing your soul into his body. It will, for a moment, become a part of him. It's the most gentle way to..." He couldn't bring himself to finish the sentence.

"To kill me," Scarlett added, trying to remain brave.

Owlen nodded, finding it increasingly difficult to put this situation into words. "Yes," he confirmed. "You'll begin to slowly fade away, and after a moment or so, your heart will stop beating."

Scarlett listened intently, clinging onto hope that this was the only way toward a life with Finn. "So, once my heart stops beating?" she inquired, trying to ignore the knots in her stomach.

"Finn will return your soul in the same way it was taken, only this time, you will have part of his as well. You'll be his creation—a part of him."

"And I'll wake up as a demon?" Scarlett tried to grasp the concept as Owlen nodded. She took a deep breath to steady herself. She couldn't deny her fear, but she would do her best to keep it hidden from Finn. The dark situation seemed a bit brighter knowing that she and Finn would be a part of each other when this was over. Soulmates.

Finn listened from a distance as their conversation grew silent. He closed his eyes for a moment, fighting back tears that threatened to escape, wiping sweat from his brow. His hands trembled as he tried to gather himself. There was no way to truly prepare for this. No way to make it easier. He would simply have to do it, for her sake.

With a deep breath, he returned to his friends, his steps heavy and hesitant. He knelt in the grass just as he did when his wings were torn from his body. To Finn, it felt very much like another piece of him was about to be torn away.

Scarlett gave Owlen a final embrace. As she squeezed him tightly, she whispered a heartfelt plea in his ear. "If this doesn't work out, please take care of him."

Owlen, feeling the weight of her words and the immense responsibility they carried, nodded with a solemn promise in his eyes. "I will, my dear, you have my word. But let's have faith that it won't come to that."

With these words, Scarlett lay down next to Finn, using her hand to gently turn his face toward hers. Her heart pounded with anxiety as they locked eyes for a brief moment. Finn leaned down to hug her tightly, his heart breaking at the thought that this could be their last embrace.

"I love you," Scarlett whispered, and in an instant, Finn's world froze. Those words. He had existed for an eternity and had never heard those words being spoken to *him*. In this critical moment when he was about to potentially lose her, they struck him deeply.

He held her close, his voice cracking as he asked, "You're able to love me, after all this?"

Scarlett, with a small, brave smile tried to lighten the heavy atmosphere. "Of course I love you—I'd die for you, remember?"

A small chuckle left Finn's lips. Her words eased some of the pain in his heart. "And I love you," he added. "I'll love you for the rest of my existence."

Owlen leaned down next to his friends as ominous clouds began swirling above them. His warm presence was always a comfort. "I'll be right beside you both, every step of the way." With gentle hands, he reached out to both of them. Their fingers intertwined, forming a trembling, but unbreakable bond of support.

As Finn prepared to take the first, fateful breath, he whispered into Scarlett's ear. "Hold on to the thought of us. I'll bring you back, I promise." With that, he closed his eyes, leaned in, and took a deep, shuddering breath. Scarlett felt a strange tug deep within her chest and she was suddenly unable to move. Tears fell freely from the corners of her eyes onto the ground below.

*This was it.*

Everything around her began to fade away, and in its place, a kaleidoscope of vivid visions began to unfold. She did her best to hold onto the thought of Finn in her mind, just as he said. His crimson eyes were gazing at her through roaring flames that were no longer threatening. A strange sense of warmth and longing spread through her lifeless body as he was making his way toward her through the fire.

Owlen appeared next, his beautiful eyes filled with kindness and wisdom. He was smiling at her as they walked, leading the way with her hand on his arm—always the perfect gentleman. She saw the garden, but not as it is now. It was whole and beautiful, with thousands of colorful flowers dancing happily in the breeze.

Finn continued to draw deep breaths while Owlen was by his side breathing deeply as well, as if to guide him through the process. As the visions began to fade, Scarlett felt a growing sense of unease. The memories of Finn and Owlen were slipping away, like grains of sand through her fingers. She desperately tried to hold onto those precious images, reaching out to them, but they drifted further and further from her grasp.

Finn's crimson eyes, once so close, became a distant point of light on the horizon. She stretched her hand toward them, but they continued to recede into the darkness. Panic welled up inside of her as the visions dissolved into... *nothing*.

Finn took one last breath, feeling Owlen's presence beside him, doing the same as an offering of silent support. Their hands were still intertwined, a lifeline connecting them to each other, and to Scarlett. As he leaned down, Finn paused for a moment, looking into Scarlett's serene face. She looked so peaceful, as if she were merely sleeping. He whispered her name gently, expecting to see a flicker of life in her eyes, a sign that she was still with them. But there was nothing—no flutter of the eyelashes, no breath escaping her lips.

Panic surged through Finn like a tidal wave, drowning reason and restraint. He nudged her desperately, as if he could coax her back to life with his touch, but she remained still, her heart silent. "Scarlett!" he cried out, his voice filled with anguish. He pulled her lifeless form into his arms, holding her close, urgently trying to revive her.

Scarlett walked through the darkness, not knowing which direction she was going. She put her hand up in front of her face and waved it frantically, but she couldn't see it, and this made her suddenly ill. Was she blind? She lowered herself to the ground, feeling for the familiar grass beneath her feet, but felt cold, hard stone instead.

"Finn! Owlen!" She called out to her friends, desperate to know where they were—where *she* was—but the silence made her ears ring and pulsate.

"Letti..Letti, it's okay. Don't be afraid."

That voice. She knew that voice. It seemed to fill the air all around her, echoing through the nothingness—a welcome sound to calm the unbearable ringing. Scarlett whipped around to see a light forming from far behind her, and in a celestial haze, stood her parents, smiling at her. Scarlett's mouth fell open as she struggled to believe what she saw. Her parents, healthy and happy, had come to find her.

In the garden, Owlen watched, his heart breaking as his dear friend tried to revive Scarlett.  But he knew the steps of this process had to be followed, and as the skies were blackening, he couldn't let Finn's despair consume them both. He placed his hands gently on Finn's tear-stained face, forcing him to meet his gaze. "Finn, look at me. Listen," Owlen urged, his voice steady and soothing. "Remember, this is part of the plan. We're here together, and you can do this. Bring her back to us. I'm right here beside you."

Finn nodded and wiped his face, attempting to collect himself. He clung to Scarlett's lifeless form, his hand trembling as he held her face. He exhaled, allowing his breath to enter her lips in a desperate attempt to bring her back.

Once.

Twice.

Three times, he tried, each breath deeper and more deter-mined than the last. But there was no response—no sign of life from the woman he loved. "Come on, come back to me," Finn pleaded, his voice choking with despair. Panic swelled within him as the billowing clouds began to consume their world.

Scarlett began walking toward her parents, their arms opening up to welcome her. They seemed so far away, but her mother's voice whispered in her ear. "You're safe now, Letti. Come home with us." Scarlett walked faster now, eager to meet their embrace. As her pace quickened, another voice came from behind her.

"Come back to me, baby. Please!" Finn's desperate cries stopped Scarlett in her tracks. "Come on, come back, please."

As Scarlett stood, searching the darkness behind her, silvery, swirling smoke began to loom in the distance. Finn's crimson eyes could be seen glowing in the billows. Owlen appeared next to him, his porcelain skin barely visible, though she could see his beautiful blue eyes shining with sadness as he watched Finn reach for her. "Please come back to me."

Beside Scarlett's body, Owlen watched with a heavy heart, realizing the weight of the situation. The bright light of hope he tried to hold onto now flickered in the face of Scarlett's lifeless state. This should have worked by now. How would he pull Finn out of the incredible darkness that would swallow him after losing the one he loved?

For now he could only offer words of encouragement. "Focus, Finn," Owlen urged, his voice unwavering, despite the grim circumstances. "Steady your breath and picture her creation in your mind. You can do this."

Finn obeyed, trying to steady his racing heart and regain control of his emotions. He pictured Scarlett's radiant smile, her beautiful eyes, her laughter. Moments they would share together when she would awaken as his demon. He breathed into her again, so deeply her chest rose and fell under the force of his breath.

But still, his efforts failed.

With mounting desperation, Finn begged Owlen for help. His voice was frantic, his crimson eyes filled with terror. "Do something, please! She's not coming back!"

Scarlett stood looking at her friends, their eyes filled with despair as they began to slowly fade away. Finn held out his hand through the silver smoke, desperate to hold onto hope that she would return to him. Panic began to set in as Scarlett had to make her choice.

She looked back at her parents, with tears in her eyes. "I'm... I'm sorry, I have to go to them. I belong with them." The words burned in her throat as she looked at their faces. They were beginning to fade faster now, and her mother's voice whispered once more in her ear.

"We love you, Letti. We'll always love you."

Finn's fingertips were barely visible now as Owlen pushed his own hand through the smoke. Scarlett gasped knowing she didn't have much time. She looked back at her parents one last time and they both smiled with understanding. She wanted to remember them this way. "I love you both. So much."

"Go on," her father urged. "They'll take care of you, but you have to hurry." He gave her a heartfelt grin, and with glistening eyes, he put his arm around his wife as they disappeared into the darkness.

Her heart splintered at the thought of losing  them again, but knowing that her parents were together and healthy gave her the peace she needed to pull herself together. She turned around and began running toward what was left of the silver haze.

Owlen felt helpless, desperately searching his mind for answers as Finn held Scarlett, sobbing. Then a burst of realization crossed his face. Without hesitation, Owlen gently took Scarlett from Finn's arms and pulled her face toward him, exhaling deeply through her lips.

In that electrifying moment, Scarlett's eyes snapped open. Her chest heaved, and she gasped for breath as life surged back into her.

Finn's relief was visible as he tried to catch his breath. He stared in wonder at the woman who returned to him from the other side of death. Without a second thought, he pulled her into a fierce kiss, tasting the sweet miracle of her return. He held her tightly, looking at Owlen, who was responsible for this miraculous revival. He couldn't help but feel an immense gratitude that words could never express. Owlen gave him a relieved smile, catching his own breath and calming his pounding heartbeat. Finn simply nodded, his eyes shimmering, silently thanking his dear friend.

Scarlett, still weak from her ordeal, fainted as she attempted to stand on her own. She needed rest. Finn gently lifted her into his arms, carrying her with the utmost of care as Owlen followed closely behind. Their steps were quiet and careful as they walked toward the cottage. They gazed up at the sky, and to their immense relief, the menacing clouds had dissipated completely. The horizon was clear, and although the land around them remained destroyed, any sign of impending danger had vanished.

Soren was finally gone—his darkness retreating back into the fiery depths from which he had emerged. Finn and Owlen exchanged expressions of sincere relief, their eyes meeting in a silent acknowledgment of their shared victory. They had succeeded, and Scarlett was now safe from Soren's grasp.

# CHAPTER SEVEN

## LIFE

Scarlett lay on the cozy bed, her eyes closed and her breathing steady. Her transformation had taken a significant toll on her, leaving her physically and emotionally drained. She slept for days on end, her body working to adjust to the immense change she had undergone. Finn and Owlen never left her side, watching over her attentively as she recovered. Finn sat on the edge of the bed, Scarlett's hand resting gently in his, while Owlen found his place in a nearby chair.

Owlen's eyes were carefully fixed on her slumbering form as a solemn realization crossed his face. "I'm really going to miss taking care of her after this," he said quietly, breaking the silence. "I was enjoying creating meals for her. Giving her anything she needed while she was human; she won't need me anymore."

Finn turned toward his friend as saw the pain in his expression. He reached over, gently grasping Owlen's fidgeting hands. "Hey... this is going to be an adjustment. We both need you more than ever right now."

Seeing that his words didn't provide the comfort he had hoped, Finn continued. "You're her best friend. She *loves* you. The only thing that will change is that now we'll have forever together."

Owlen looked up at that, a small spark of hope fluttering across his face. "I hope you're right."

Finn squeezed Owlen's hand and flashed a grin. "Aren't I always right?"

Owlen chuckled softly and squeezed Finn's hand in return. "Thank you," he whispered sincerely.

"Are you kidding? *You're* the one who brought her back to me. We both owe you so much." Finn paused to ponder in silence. After a moment, he took a deep breath and asked the questions that have been on his mind since the moment of Scarlett's return. "So, how did you know what to do, anyway? I mean, you were the one who saved her... how is that possible when I'm the one who took her soul? What happened out there?"

The questions startled Owlen. He closed his eyes for a moment, hiding the panic that came with divulging the truth. A truth that would change everything. *How* he saved

Scarlett was simple. He was next to Finn, breathing deeply with him, and as Scarlett's soul left her body, he unknowingly claimed a part as well. Once he realized this, saving her became his commitment. But as he breathed life back into her, a part of his own soul was given to her in return. Half-angel, half-demon. Her creation wasn't the issue here. This beautiful creature lying before them was the result of their love. A perfect mix of Heaven and Hell.

What came next, however, was something that Owlen didn't expect. The lifeline they created through their interlocked hands that day had caused Finn and Owlen to exchange pieces of their immortal souls as well. This shared connection between their three bodies brought forth a whirlwind of emotion that Owlen couldn't foresee. A newfound desire for them both. A deep love that surpassed the bond of friendship.

Scarlett's presence, her laughter, Finn's touch, their history —they had all become precious to him in a way he couldn't explain. Although he couldn't deny the way his heart quickened at the thought of his soul mates, he didn't dare express it. For now he could only remain on the outside looking in, as painful as that might be, to avoid disrupting the delicate balance of the life they created together.

He looked up to meet Finn's crimson eyes, and his mind searched quickly for a response. But as his mouth opened to speak, Scarlett stirred in her sleep, grabbing their attention. Owlen stood up from his chair and knelt on the floor next to the bed. He began gently stroking Scarlett's long brown hair, lulling her back to sleep. Finn placed a hand on

Owlen's shoulder and stood up from the bed, stretching his legs. He watched Owlen for a moment, tending to Scarlett with an almost obsessive attention to detail. The angel's gentle demeanor had shifted into a protective guardian, ensuring Scarlett's every comfort. It was heartwarming to see.

All of his attention had been focused so closely on Scarlett's recovery, but seeing Owlen's devoted care in that moment gave him a feeling he couldn't explain. It was as if a veil had been lifted from his eyes, revealing the depths of Owlen's kindness and the warmth of his gentle smile—things Finn realized he had taken for granted. An overwhelming surge flooded within Finn—a desire to see happiness reflected in Owlen's blue eyes. Although nothing he could do seemed like enough, he felt a longing to repay his dear friend for his unwavering support.

An idea struck him like a bolt of inspiration. What better way to express his gratitude than to restore what had been destroyed? With a smile Finn squeezed Owlen's shoulder gently. "Hey angel," he began softly. "Would you stay with her for a while? I'm going to get some air for a bit."

Owlen looked at him with relief in his eyes. He had managed to avoid any further inquiry from Finn for now. "Yes, of course. She'll be in good hands, don't worry."

With that, Finn left the cottage and ventured into the garden. A rainbow of birds were resting in what was left of the tree branches, filling the air with their evening lullaby. The warm glow of the setting sun was stretching long shadows across the demolished landscape. He walked among the twisted remains of Owlen's beloved plants, their petals burned by Soren's wrath.

This was an unconventional plan. Tending to flowers and making things beautiful were typically out of character for a demon. But nonetheless, he had a deep seated need to lift the lingering shadow of dark magic that clung to Owlen's home —to *their* home, and so he went to work.

Finn's hands moved expertly through the evening air, his fingers tracing invisible patterns as he focused carefully on the garden's restoration. Each gesture was filled with the desire to mend what had been broken—to bring back the serenity that Owlen treasured so dearly.

First he tackled the huge crevice that had marred the expanse of the garden, a stark reminder of the chaos that had unfolded. With a wave of his hand, the earth shifted, rocks and soil flowing like water to fill the abyss. A beautiful pathway took its place, stretching from the cottage to the horizon. It was tedious work, ensuring every piece fit seamlessly, every blade of grass perfectly placed.

The flowers were next, their vibrant colors returning in a rainbow of life. Finn could feel Owlen's presence in every petal, every leaf. With gentle care, he coaxed them back from the brink, nurturing their growth as if they were gentle souls in need of protection.

The dead leaves and broken branches that littered the ground dissolved into dust and disappeared at his command. New foliage burst forth in vibrant greens and deep browns. The trees, once scorched and bare, now stretched their full limbs toward the stars. Birds rested comfortably on their newly restored perches, chirping songs of gratitude to the demon who rejuvenated their home.

As the Moon climbed higher in the sky, Finn now focused on the cottage. The broken remnants of the door were replaced with fresh, sturdy wood. The windows were now clear and unbroken, reflecting the Moon and Earth in their splendor. Further up the path, Finn stood before the damaged picnic table that Owlen had created for Scarlett. It was nestled among a bed of beautiful purple flowers, now trampled and wilted. With a deep breath, he extended his hand and with a wave, the splintered wood of the table began to knit itself back together, the cracks sealing seamlessly as if they had never been there.

Next, he turned his attention to the flowers. With a gentle motion of his hand, the wilted petals stood upright, regaining their vibrant purple hue. The crushed stems straightened, and the flowers bloomed just as they did with Owlen's touch.

Finally, Finn stepped back, his breath catching as he surveyed their transformed world. The once-shattered sanctuary was now thriving again, bathed in the silvery glow of the Moon. It was as if time had been rewound, erasing the scars of that fateful event. A sense of satisfaction and relief washed over him. He couldn't wait to see Owlen's reaction, to witness the joy in his friend's eyes when he discovered that life had been given to his garden once again. With a weary, but contented smile, Finn returned to the cottage, ready to share his gift with Owlen.

The moonlight filtered through the bedroom window, bringing its soft, dreamy glow into the quiet room. Scarlett and Owlen were both in a peaceful slumber. Owlen was still knelt beside the bed, his head resting next to Scarlett's as he slept, holding her hand as if to offer comfort even in her sleep. They looked like two perfectly contented souls, unaware of the transformed world outside. Finn smiled as he leaned down to kiss Scarlett's forehead. She stirred slightly, but remained in the peaceful embrace of her dreams, pulling Owlen's hand closer to her.

With the utmost care, Finn settled into the chair next to the bed. He reached over and gently brushed the golden strands of hair from Owlen's forehead. He had never realized how striking Owlen truly was. His porcelain skin was beautiful in the moonlight and Finn had to stop himself, so as to not wake his friend with his touch. An overwhelming sense of fulfillment washed over him. With the weight of their recent ordeal lifted, and Scarlett's recovering underway, the three of them could finally embrace the future together.

The night had passed peacefully, and as the first rays of dawn peeked into the room, Owlen stirred from his rest. His eyes opened to see Finn, who had been keeping vigil all night, watching over the two in a quiet devotion. "Good morning," Owlen greeted Finn with a smile. He turned to check on Scarlett, gently placing her hand back at her side.

Finn returned the smile. "Good morning," he replied in a soft voice. "I have something to show you, if you don't mind. Outside."

"Of course," Owlen said with an inquiring look. His gaze shifted once more toward Scarlett, who lay asleep, her breathing steady and peaceful. He stood up and hesitated for a moment, second-guessing his decision. He didn't want to leave her side.

"We won't be long, I promise," Finn reassured him, gesturing toward the door.

As the two of them stepped outside, Owlen was met with a sight that left him utterly speechless. The ruins of the garden had been turned into a breathtaking paradise, even more beautiful than he remembered.  The crevice that divided their world was gone, replaced by a path lined with beautiful flowers, their vibrant petals swaying in the gentle morning breeze. His breath caught in his throat as his trembling hand reached down to touch the delicate petals. He couldn't stop the tears from welling up in his blue eyes.

He turned to Finn, unable to find the words to express the depth of his emotions. For a moment, silence hung between them, and then Owlen managed to whisper, his voice choked with gratitude. "Thank you."

Finn's response was simple, but heartfelt. "It was nothing," accompanied by the smirk that Owlen knew all too well. "Just wanted to make it *pretty* for you again, or whatever," he added, casually. Owlen wrapped his arms around Finn in a warm embrace. They held each other tightly, conveying all the feelings that words could not express. It was a hug of gratitude, affection, and something more that had grown between them.

As the two walked through the door of the bedroom, they were greeted by a delightful surprise—Scarlett had awakened. She was sitting up in bed, admiring the restored garden through the window. She looked at them and smiled, speaking to Finn. "You fixed it! It's gorgeous!" They both rushed to her side with visible relief. They enveloped her in a loving embrace, Finn on one side and Owlen on the other. Their joy overflowed when they realized that she had indeed fully recovered. Tears of happiness glistened in their eyes as she whispered. "I'm fine. Thank you both for taking care of me. I know you were beside me the whole time. How long was I out, anyway?"

"Twelve days," Owlen answered quickly.

Finn, his emotions brimming over, touched her cheek with his thumb. "But days don't matter anymore," he whispered as he leaned in to kiss her. His lips brushed hers in a kiss that was both gentle and passionate, one that now held the promise of an eternity together.

Owlen watched quietly from their side with a soft smile. Although his heart ached beneath the surface, he understood the significance of this kiss. It was a symbol of their unity, their shared journey of defeating the odds of death, and the profound connection between his friends that he helped create.

When the kiss finally broke, they remained close, their foreheads touching. "Your eyes are absolutely stunning," Finn whispered. His words drew the attention of Owlen as well. He leaned over to look at Scarlett, his gaze lingering perhaps a bit longer than intended before a faint blush colored his cheeks.

Scarlett, a little confused by the sudden interest, stood up and walked to the bathroom mirror. As she saw her reflection, a gasp escaped her lips. While she slept, her eyes transformed into the most beautiful shade of purple, reminiscent of the Royal Amethysts that Owlen planted especially for her. Rushing back into the bedroom, her heart racing with excitement, she threw her arms around Finn with gratitude. "Thank you! They're incredible! I love them!"

Finn shook his head softly. "It wasn't me. Owlen ended up bringing you back. We were very lucky to have him there."

Scarlet turned her gaze toward Owlen, searching his eyes for confirmation. "Is that true?" she asked, her voice filled with curiosity.

Owlen shifted uncomfortably under her captivating stare, his cheeks turning a deeper shade of red. "Well, you see, it's a bit complicated," he stammered, attempting to avoid more discussion.

Finn couldn't help but chuckle at Owlen's flustered reaction. "He's just being modest," he teased. "Our angel did something extraordinary to save you, whatever it was."

Scarlett smiled warmly at Owlen, taking his hand in hers. "Thank you," she said, her eyes still fixed on his. "I couldn't have asked for a better friend."

Owlen cleared his throat, his embarrassment slowly fading into a pleased smile. "You're very welcome, my dear."

"So," Finn spoke up, "What would you like to do now on your first official day as a demon?"

"Anything but sleep," Scarlett said with a laugh. She pulled Finn to his feet and wrapped her arms around his waist, resting her head on his chest. "I just want things to go back to how they were, before Soren, you know? If that's okay."

Finn leaned down, kissing the top of her head as he pulled her closer. "Well, good news—you'll never have to sleep again. Let's go outside. You can see the improvements I made," he smirked.

He walked quietly by Scarlett's side as she explored the renewed world around her. He watched with a smile as she experienced the breathtaking sights and sounds of her new existence. Warmth still flowed through her veins, just as it always had, and the delightful feeling of the sun on her skin brought a sense of comfort and familiarity—a reminder that she was still herself, despite the changes she felt.

The most immediate difference was her lack of hunger. After sleeping for twelve days, she would expect to wake up weak and ravenous, but it wasn't so, and the sudden realization of no longer enjoying Owlen's exquisite food caused a tinge of sadness. She couldn't help but wonder if Owlen felt the same way about missing out on those moments together. Noticing that Finn was studying her expression, she shook the thought from her head, and allowed the strange, new beauty of her surroundings fill her.

Colors were more vivid and alive, like her violet eyes were seeing the world through a new perspective. She gasped at the rich, deep shades of green in every leaf, the vibrant hues of every petal, the brilliant blue of the sky. The air was alive with a symphony of life. Birds and insects seemed to be singing for her, alone, their delicate chirping and buzzing reaching her ears from across the expanse. The natural world was celebrating her awakening. She couldn't explain her transformation, but she embraced it fully, thankful for this rare gift she was given to experience everything anew.

Finn wrapped his arms around her from behind, pressing his lips against her ear. "Nice, huh?" he whispered. His breath, warm and inviting, sent an eruption of goosebumps across her skin. His sensual voice was electrifying, awakening every nerve in her body. She turned to him, her eyes locking onto his with an intensity that her mortal self had never experienced. His crimson eyes, which had always held a certain magnetism, now smoldered with an irresistible force.

"Can we go to our place?" she asked him, clearing her throat. It felt like a lifetime since they lay together under the sprawling tree near the stream. There they would talk about endless topics, sharing their thoughts, stories, fears. It had been a place where their hearts were mended and their lips first met.

He extended his hand to her, his fingers entwining with hers as he led her to their cherished spot. The grass felt cool and inviting beneath them as they settled down, their bodies fitting together like pieces of a puzzle as the hours passed them by. Scarlett was nestled in the crook of Finn's arm, her head resting on his chest as the evening sky began to cover them like a blanket. His heartbeat echoed in her ear, a steady rhythm that had become a soothing lullaby. This would have lulled her to sleep as a human, but now she could take in every beat, every breath, without missing a thing.

Finn's fingers gently traced patterns on Scarlett's back as she lay there, soaking in her embrace as the night unfolded. The Moon and Earth hung above them, shining brightly among a canvas of stars. Scarlett's thoughts began to wander as she watched them and finally, she broke the silence, turning to look at Finn. "Do you ever think that maybe I'm holding you guys back?"

Finn's brows furrowed in confusion. "What? What do you mean *holding us back*?"

"It's just... the two of you used to go everywhere together. I've heard so many stories about the places you've been, things you've done. Now it seems like you're just *stuck* here... because of me."

Finn sat up, his eyes meeting Scarlett's with a soft, reassuring smile. He reached out, brushing her hair from her face. "Listen," he began, his voice gentle, but resolute, "you've never held us back, not for a moment. You've added something to our lives, something incredible and irreplaceable." Finn leaned in, pressing a tender kiss to her lips. "It's not where we go or what we do, anymore—it's who we're with, and as long as you're here, this is where we want to be."

Scarlett's eyes shimmered with emotion as she absorbed his words. She reached out, her fingers tracing the contours of Finn's face. "Thank you," she whispered, trying to tame her goosebumps. "I'll be able to travel with you both, eventually, right? After I get better at things, I mean?"

Finn looked back up at the stars. It was difficult to tell her that, while he and Owlen would never feel *stuck* with her, they would, indeed, be stuck in the present with her. "I don't think so." Scarlett's silent reaction told him that he should explain. "Demons can't travel through time like Owlen and I can. The only reason I can is because I was created as an angel, and *chose* to become a demon. My creation still allows me to."

"Why can't I, I mean, why can't *demons* do what you do?" The disappointment in Scarlett's voice was heartbreaking and Finn knew he couldn't bend these rules for her. So he attempted to lighten the mood.

"Can you imagine a bunch of demons going through time, messing everything up? Earth would have turned out far worse than you left it, if that were possible."

Scarlett gave a faint smile and squeezed him tightly. She turned back to look at their cottage. Candlelight flicked from within, but the shades were drawn. "What do you think Owlen's doing? Should we check on him?"

The mention of Owlen's name brought a bittersweet pang to Finn's heart. He hadn't seen their friend outside of their cottage all day, which was unusual, to say the least. A subtle sense of sadness swelled up within him, like a missing piece in the puzzle of their existence. Since the day he brought Scarlett to their world, Owlen had always been nearby, offering a smile, even if from afar.

He glanced at Scarlett, her eyes filled with genuine concern for Owlen. Finn could understand her worry, as he shared it. But he also knew that their friend might need some time alone after Scarlett's recovery. The events of the last weeks had been emotionally taxing for all of them. He gave Scarlett a reassuring smile. "I'm sure he's tired of us. He's probably enjoying a bit of solitude. We'll give him some space. He'll join us when he's ready."

Scarlett nodded, nestling closer to Finn, though concern still lingered in her eyes. While she couldn't help but wonder about Owlen's seclusion, she felt comfort in Finn's presence. Even though their time was now endless, she was determined to cherish every moment they had, whether in the company of their beloved angel, or in the embrace of each other's arms.

# CHAPTER EIGHT

## SECRETS

The passage of time seemed to blur as days unfolded seamlessly into one another. Finn and Scarlett spent every second together in the wake of Scarlett's newfound immortality. They were like two stars in their own little universe, orbiting each other with an irresistible gravitational pull. Finn's realization that he would never have to endure the pain of losing Scarlett again gave him an immense sense of gratitude, and every moment together was a precious gem that he was determined to collect. However, even with the euphoria of emerging from the turmoil they endured, an unspoken void was beginning to grow between them.

Owlen's absence had become like a shadow that slowly encroached on their happiness. Scarlett often found herself staring at the cottage door, waiting for him to emerge with a smile, ready to join them as though nothing had happened. She would gladly welcome him.

She tried reassuring herself that their friend just needed some time alone, just as Finn said. *Time to heal*, whatever that meant. She trusted Finn's judgment and kept her distance. After all, he knew Owlen better than anyone else. Still, the doubt lingered in her mind, and she couldn't help but wonder if Owlen's solitude was masking something deeper. He was too precious to have such pain in his heart, and Scarlett's worry grew more with each passing day.

Finn's inner turmoil was no less significant. He had pushed Owlen away, thinking it must be what their friend wanted. What he needed. But the weight of Owlen's absence was crushing. He couldn't make sense of it. He had spent countless years seeing Owlen only sporadically—meeting him when his duties of being a demon allowed it. But now, an immense sense of loss weighed on him. Owlen was merely a stone's throw away from him, but he felt further from him than he ever had.

He ached to know what they had done to make Owlen keep his distance for so long. Any minute now he could emerge from their home and end this pain for all of them. So why wouldn't he? During the course of their friendship, Finn had witnessed the angel's kindness and affection given so freely, which is what made Owlen's withdrawal all the more incomprehensible.

Finn did his best to reassure Scarlett that the three of them would be together soon enough. He hid his pain, trying to protect her from the guilt that was overtaking him. But during their nights together, the shades of the cottage window remained pulled, and the sadness in Finn's usually vibrant eyes was evident. Their time apart became a crushing weight on his chest, making it nearly impossible to breathe, and each thought of Owlen only tightened the grip around his heart. As the days passed by, he felt as though he had been cut adrift from the anchor he had in his world with Owlen, and was floating further and further away from shore.

The day of Scarlett's awakening was a flurry of joy and relief for Owlen. He watched her from afar as she immersed herself in the gift of immortality. Her bond with Finn was an undeniable force. Sacrifice, death, and then life; their love could clearly withstand anything. It was beautiful, but also heartbreaking. He was standing on the outside of something so precious to him, yet just beyond his reach.

He would steal glimpses of his friends from the safety of his four walls, until the pain he felt as he witnessed each kiss, each touch, became unbearable. Just days ago, he felt like an inseparable part of them, but now, life with his soul mates was like a cruel mirage that teased him from afar.

Although accidental, Owlen was wholly aware that he was responsible for his situation. His decision to distance himself wasn't made out of spite or anger, but as a desperate need to protect his own heart. He knew this was his own struggle, his own dilemma. His friends had done nothing to deserve the isolation he had imposed on them, but he felt helpless to do otherwise. He wouldn't be able to conceal the heartbreak that surged within him each time Scarlett would take Finn's hand, and not his. Every time Finn would stroke her long brown hair, while he watched from the side. The two of them deserved a chance to let their love flourish without the shadow of his pain over them.

Owlen missed them both terribly, and the loneliness that began building within the cottage walls was suffocating. In the evenings he would pull the shades down tight to avoid the temptation of watching them hold each other in the intimacy of the Moon's glow. When the sun would rise, he woke up and began to busy himself, passing the time until he could sleep again. It seemed like an endless cycle of avoiding pain—a routine he welcomed reluctantly.

Although seclusion within the confines of the cottage was wearing on him, the thought of traveling and leaving his friends behind was never an option. The bond he shared with Finn and Scarlett was a tremendous force that tethered him, pulling at him constantly. He could never sever that connection, nor could he bear the thought of truly being apart from them. And so, rather than venturing away, he chose to retreat into his own space, while still remaining as close to them as he could manage.

Seated in his living room chair, accompanied only by candlelight, Owlen immersed himself in his books, reading volume after volume of poetry and essays, in hopes of escaping the persistent ache in his heart. With every turn of the page, he searched for comfort in the written word. Some piece of wisdom that would help him get from one day to the next. He sought to lose himself in the pain of others before him. Those who wrote about their own accounts of unrequited love and tragic loss. His books quickly became a precious sanctuary, shielding him from what lay beyond his isolation, even if only for a little while.

But inevitably, the silence would grab hold of him again. It was in those quiet moments when the ache of their absence became too much to bear. Although he was in refuge, he secretly wished his friends would come to him; that they would break through the walls he had built around himself, ending the misery of their separation.

It had been well over a week since Scarlett saw Owlen's face. Her eyes were trained on the familiar cottage door, just as they had been each morning since her change. In days long gone, before complications and misunderstandings polluted their bond, Owlen would wake up with the sunrise, coming outside to greet their world with his infectious smile. The sunrise had come and gone, however, and the door remained closed. The candlelight flickering in the night had been the only promising sign of life from within the dark windows.

Scarlett had endured the silence and separation long enough. She needed to see Owlen, to reconnect, to heal the wounds that had seemingly formed between them. She stood up abruptly, her frustration evident as she hastily dusted off grass from the back of her pants. The sudden movement startled Finn, who had been sitting beside her, quietly watching the horizon change from darkness to daylight. He rose to his feet, helping her as she straightened her clothes.

"I can't take this any longer." Anger simmered in her voice. "I know you said he needs time, but he's had enough time. I've been through this too—we both have, and we aren't shutting *him* out. This is ridiculous." She began walking toward the cottage when Finn reached for her shoulder, stopping her.

"Wait," he quickly blurted, but as Scarlett turned to look at him, she saw a sense of relief that changed his worried expression. Her taking charge in that moment had made him feel a little silly that he hadn't done this himself, but he was grateful, nonetheless. The weight of whatever Owlen was going through had affected them all and that was possibly about to change. He kissed her forehead as he squeezed her shoulders. "Go on," he encouraged. "I'll come in later after you both have had some time to talk."

Scarlett's determination led her to the cottage, but as she stood staring at the front door, she had to settle the butterflies in her stomach. It was illogical, she knew. This was Owlen, her dearest friend. The person who always knew the right thing to say in any situation. But this situation was different, more complicated. She had no idea why, but the need to see Owlen was deeper than she had let on to Finn. It was more than the words they'd exchange. It was like a broken piece of herself was waiting inside those walls, and she was here to put it back together. Although Scarlett was on the outside, just the act of standing on the other side of the door from Owlen brought her a sense of peace and quiet reassurance.

Inside, Owlen had reluctantly settled into his new routine. The rising sun, once an invitation to a new day with his friends, was now an unwelcome reminder of loneliness. Instead of stepping outside, he now sank into one of the plush armchairs that furnished the living room. Books placed neatly into stacks now surrounded Owlen, offering him a way to temporarily escape the unbearable emptiness he felt.

Each new day brought the same internal struggle, to reach out or remain hidden in his emotional fortress. He didn't know how long he could continue this self-imposed torture, but the thought of facing his friends as if nothing had happened felt like a hot iron in his throat. Pretending as if it didn't shatter his heart every time he saw them together laughing, kissing, and sharing moments without him.

Owlen picked up the closest book, its cover tattered and worn from the countless times he had treasured it. It was far too special to simply repair into new condition with magic. A beautiful velvet ribbon cascaded gracefully from between the aged pages, its crimson color as rich and passionate as the verse it marked. He stroked the ribbon gently as he read the cover once more. *Prose For The Heart: Verses Of Love And Longing* was etched in beautiful calligraphy. The faded words would be nearly impossible to read by anyone who hadn't studied the cover time and time again.

As he opened the book, he heard it—a sound that sent his heart racing, and emotions flooding through him like a tidal wave.

A knock at the door.

He held his breath and the book in his hands was now forgotten on the floor as the world around him stopped in its tracks. The sound was so faint, that for a moment he thought maybe it was some cruel joke his mind was playing on him. His heartbeat, now pounding in his chest, could most certainly be mistaken for a knock at the door.

A second knock came, undeniably real this time. Owlen tore from his chair, disoriented in a mix of nervousness and excitement. He approached the door with cautious, yet quick steps and the feeling seemed to leave his fingertips as he reached for the handle. When he swung the door open, it was Scarlett who stood before him, framed in the gentle daylight. Her amethyst eyes met his gaze, and his heart surged at the sight of her. The longing to see her beautiful face had been so overwhelming, that for a moment all he could do was stare.

He began to move forward for a long overdue hug, but his joy was short-lived. Scarlett held up her hand and stepped back, rejecting his embrace. A confused expression crossed her face as her eyes darted past him, focused on Owlen's surroundings—specifically on the towering books that now filled the small room.

A wave of self-consciousness washed over Owlen as he was reminded about how isolated he had become, and how the state of their cottage must look. "Scarlett, my dear," he greeted her. "It's been quite some time. I'm..."

"*Reading*?" The anger Owlen had feared she was feeling when she rejected his hug was evident now. "You've been reading? Owlen, it's been *days*. We were worried about you, and this whole time you've been in here relaxing like nothing happened?"

Owlen found it difficult to look into her eyes now. Her look of disappointment would crush him if he weren't careful. "I'm so sorry, my dear. It really isn't what it looks like, I promise. I guess I've just been battling my own thoughts."

"Yeah, Finn said you needed some time alone, but this whole thing is ridiculous, don't you think? I mean, you two are impossible. I don't even know what the problem is and it seems like I'm the only one willing to fix things. Don't you want to?"

"Of course," his voice trembled again. "I want very badly for things to be normal again." Scarlett could see the pain in his eyes as he was fighting back tears, and her expression softened. She got her point across, but seeing Owlen hurt was not what she wanted. She stepped forward and wrapped her arms around his waist. His tears fell freely now as he squeezed her tightly—no longer starved for touch, and rested his head on hers. "I'm so sorry," he whispered.

The two friends held each other for a moment, and in that silence, Scarlett's anger melted away. She noticed how different it felt hugging Owlen than Finn. When her demon would wrap his arms around her, she could feel his lean, muscular form surrounding her like stone—powerful and protective. Owlen's embrace, on the other hand, was softer, and comforting against her skin.

The scent of old books and a hint of vanilla surrounded her, a stark contrast to the scent of leather and smoke associated with Finn. His hug was tender and soothing, and for a moment, she closed her eyes, letting his gentle arms surround her like a comforting blanket—much needed after his recent distance. She didn't want to let him go, pulling him in tighter one last time before finally breaking the silence. "So, should we go inside?"

Owlen cleared his throat, "Of course. I feel just terrible that you felt the need to knock. This is your *home.*"

"I know, but we were giving you some privacy." Scarlett said with a shrug.  Owlen opened the door, ushering her inside. He glanced around, hoping to at least catch a glimpse of Finn before closing the door. "He'll be here in a little while," Scarlett offered, when she noticed his curious search. "He said he wanted to give us some time to talk first."

"Right. Very, well then. Let's have a seat." Owlen guided her carefully around the stacks and led her to one of the plush armchairs, then took his place across from her. "So, please tell me, how are you adjusting?"

"Okay, I guess," Scarlett looked down at her fidgeting hands. "I mean, It's kind of disappointing though. I can't do any of the things that Finn can do. I have purple eyes, and my senses are heightened a little. Other than that, I feel kind of boring, compared to him."

Her words caught Owlen by surprise. How could she possibly see herself as boring? Just being alone with her now had stirred emotions within him that he never thought possible. He wanted so deeply to tell her how much he cherished her presence. How the sight of her made his knees buckle—thank goodness he was sitting down. His throat burned at the thought of saying what was on his mind, so instead, he safely offered words of comfort. "Being able to do those things will come with time. I'll do my best to help you. It would be a pleasure, actually."

Scarlett nodded with a soft smile. "I'd like that." She looked around the tiny room and took a deep breath, settling back into her chair. "It feels good to be in here again. I know it hasn't been *that* long, but I missed it."

Owlen looked at the books stacked around their chairs, slightly embarrassed. "I'll get everything back in order," he said, although quickly stopping himself from tidying up with a wave of his hand. Scarlett had just expressed her worry about not being able to do magic, and he definitely did not want to seem insensitive to that. "So, are you feeling well rested?" he asked, in an attempt to change the subject.

"I am. Actually, It's been strange not needing to sleep. I honestly don't know what Finn did with all this spare time over the years. It's definitely an adjustment." Scarlett looked at Owlen with genuine curiosity. "So, why is it that *you* have to sleep, but we don't?"

Owlen looked down at his own fidgeting hands now, thinking of how to answer her.

"I'm sorry," she said, thinking she may have offended him. "I didn't mean to be rude. I was just wondering."

"You weren't being rude, my dear," Owlen said with a gentle smile, but sadness was still evident in his blue eyes. "Your question just took me back to a very long time ago, to a time I had done my best to forget. Tell me, did Finn ever explain to you about how things were before he became a demon?"

Scarlett shook her head with a solemn expression. "He doesn't like to talk about it."

Owlen nodded with a silent understanding, then sat up in his chair, thinking. After a few moments of careful contemplation, he broke the silence. "Well, I'd like to tell you about it now, if you don't mind. I think it's time, and I believe it will help you understand us both a bit more when you hear our history." Scarlett sat up as well, her interest piqued.

"As you know," Owlen began, "Finn and I were both created as angels, about six-thousand years ago." A small grin crossed Owlen's face. "He was *Finneas* to me back then, and I was *Owlennian*. We were entrusted with some of the most sacred roles in creation, and it brought us immeasurable joy. We were there when the first stars twinkled in the sky, when the oceans first stirred with life, when the first breath of wind whispered through the trees..."

He paused, then a shadow passed over his features as he continued. "But as time went on, our duties became more *complicated*. Earth became more populated and we were tasked with things that tested our beliefs. Doubt crept into our hearts and flooded our minds, and we began to question our very existence. If we were created to *create* then why were we expected to do such unimaginable things?

"We were torn between duty and conscience. Questioning such things was strictly forbidden, and so we created Luminara as a place where we could stay hidden and freely discuss matters, such as our creator's true intentions." Owlen paused once more, pleasantly remembering a time when the night belonged to the two of them, before everything changed.

"So you both were banished forever because you had *doubts*?" Scarlett's expression was a mix of disbelief and anger.

"Eventually, yes," Owlen answered, sorrowfully. "Although Luminara was carefully hidden, we couldn't hide what lay in our hearts, and even deep within our minds. Our suspicions were easily seen, and we were judged harshly, without any chance for redemption."

"And that's when Finn became a demon, right?"

"He was very angry, and chose to separate himself from our creator as much as possible. He began to search the depths of the night for a way to lead him far away from who he was, and..." Owlen looked down, his eyes full of regret. "That's when he found out about Soren. The nights he spent by my side were now spent in the shadows, attempting to work his way further into the grasp of Hell, until he was working for Soren, himself."

Scarlett's eyes filled with sadness at the thought of her demon going through the pain of finding his place. Working for the same monster who almost killed her, who disfigured Finn and crushed his wings into dust. He wasn't the same demon anymore.

Owlen watched her beautiful eyes fight back tears, and he almost forgot his words. He cleared his throat, bringing himself back. "While Finn was welcomed into Soren's... *fellowship*," Owlen's lips pursed at the word, "I came here, waiting for him to return to me. I visited him occasionally, mostly in secret, but at night, I was alone. The world here slept, so I slept as well, just to pass the time until morning. Although our world here is very small, I ensured that time would pass the same as it does on Earth, so I would always know when it was night there. It helped me feel connected to him, I suppose."

"I'm so sorry, Owlen. It must have been horrible, being separated like that; being alone for so long, waiting for him."

The sadness in her eyes as she felt sorry for him made it difficult for Owlen to look at her, but as he thought about Finn returning, carrying Scarlett under his wings, he smiled. "The wait was worth it."

"I hope so." Scarlett blushed, slightly.

"The truth is, Finn was never angry that he was expelled from Heaven. I could see into his heart—into the depths of his mind, just as our creator could. He was angry because *I* was expelled. He thought of me as the best person he knew. *Pure and good,* he would think to himself. He felt that I didn't deserve what had happened."

"You didn't," Scarlett agreed.

"Thank you, my dear. It has been quite difficult to come to terms with the truth, though. The reason he chose Hell was because of *me*. He never wanted me to find out, and I never told him that I knew. I would appreciate it if it could stay between us."

"I promise," Scarlett assured him. "Can I ask you something, while Finn isn't here?"

Owlen's face grew hot at the thought of what she might ask. The panic of needing to explain the events of her death, the details of her creation, crept in, and he tried to calm himself by taking a deep breath. He attempted to sound casual. "Of course, my dear," he managed.

"I feel kind of silly asking this, because I don't want it to seem like I'm not grateful for my life now, but the reason I don't have wings... is it because Finn doesn't?"

With a silent sigh of relief, Owlen thought carefully. He wasn't ready to divulge the entire truth yet, so he chose his words cautiously before answering. "That *is* a possibility. I know it seems unfortunate, but we can't be entirely sure yet. It's also quite possible that your wings could come to you after some time, appearing when you need them, just as Finn's did. Just as mine do. Only time can tell."

"It doesn't really matter to me, I was just curious, I guess. I didn't want to ask Finn, though, you know?"

"Yes I do. I've kept mine concealed since he lost his, just out of respect, I suppose. Even as a demon he had the most beautiful wings. It was such a terrible shame to see them destroyed."

Scarlett looked down at her hands, hiding the pain in her eyes, and Owlen quickly tried to remedy her guilt. "But as I said before, he would do it again in an instant. I know it."

Scarlett nodded, knowing Owlen was right. Finn would willingly be torn to shreds if it meant saving his friends. His unconditional love for them both was a gift, freely given, that she would never take for granted. Realizing that she had been staring off, Scarlett sat up, blinking her eyes back into focus. "So," she said, shifting her attention to the books around her. "Will you read something to me?"

"Of course, my dear," Owlen answered with a surprised smile. "What do you have in mind?"

"Anything," she shrugged, "Whichever book is your favorite."

"Oh, it would be difficult to choose a favorite. I have so many." His eyes searched the room and landed on the small, familiar book at his feet. He picked it up and placed it in his lap, gently stroking the cover. How would Scarlett react if he read something so personal... so *romantic*? Anxiety loomed in his chest as he looked up at her. "Actually, there is a poem in here that reminds me of you, if you'd like to hear it."

This surprised Scarlett, and she had to calm a sudden knot in her stomach. "Sure," she nodded.

Owlen cleared his throat, and gave himself a moment for the pink to fade from his cheeks. He opened the book to the page marked by the beautiful, crimson ribbon. He placed the ribbon gently across his knee, brushing his fingers across the velvety material, which caused inexplicable goosebumps to sweep across Scarlett's skin. She watched intently as his beautiful blue eyes moved slowly across the faded pages as he read, and she found it difficult to focus on the words.

*"In a garden where foliage twists and winds,*

*She moves like a vision, a heavenly kind."*

Scarlett watched the gentle rise and fall of his chest with each verse.

*"Her hair, a waterfall of chestnut streams,*

*Entangled in the breeze, igniting dreams.*

*Each strand a whisper of fragrant desire,*

*In this garden of Eden, our hearts set fire."*

His voice was soothing, yet captivating. But as she fixed her gaze on Owlen's lips, the sound around her began to fade into a hum. Her eyes followed his form down to his fingertips, and as they gently glided along, following each word, her heart began to pound, drowning out the sound of his voice.

How long had he been reading? She had no idea. *What are you doing? Look away, you idiot,* she thought, but she hung onto his every movement as if she were in a trance.

Owlen's voice slowly returned to her.

*"As we entwine in this hidden embrace,*

*Petals encircle us, like a tender lace.*

*She leans closer, her lips softly near,*

*Alone in our garden, passion is nothing to fear."*

He hesitated for a moment before looking up to gauge Scarlett's reaction, and his breath caught in his chest when realized that she was staring at him, tracing his features from his eyes, down to his lips, then back to his eyes. She opened her mouth to speak, but just before the words could find their way out, she was snapped from her thoughts.

"Long time, angel. Did you miss me?" Owlen slammed his book shut and jumped up at Finn's sudden appearance.

"When did you get here?" Scarlett stood up as well, and wrapped her arms tightly around Finn's waist. She was glad to see him, and did her best to conceal her guilt about what just happened, whatever it was.

"I knocked, but nobody answered, so I let myself in. I missed you." He leaned down to kiss her and the warmth of his lips relieved her turmoil. "What's wrong with you, angel? You look terrified."

Owlen stood before him, his eyes wide. Beads of sweat glistened on his porcelain skin as he mustered up the courage to finally speak. "We need to talk."

# CHAPTER NINE

## BENEATH

**M**orvina licked her bony thumb and flipped through the files of one of the many cabinets in the Infernal Archives. With a hurried huff, she forced the drawer closed and opened the next, which screeched loudly in protest. She turned to ensure the room was still empty after the noise. Flickering torches provided intermittent bursts of light, casting long, dancing shadows that mocked her caution.

Confirming that she was still alone, she continued her search. Squinting through the dim lighting, she finally found what she was looking for, deep in the rusted drawer etched with the letter *I*. She gave a satisfied sigh and quickly pulled two files from their place. The sign above her gave an ominous warning in the flames: *Altering These Documents*

*In Any Way Is Strictly Forbidden.* Morvina rolled her pulled-back eyes and gave a dismissive "Hmph" through her pursed lips.

With her prizes secured, Morvina turned and walked out of the Archives, slowing to an uncomfortable pace to avoid the conspicuous echo from her shoes. She made her way down a series of hallways which were seemingly abandoned by the usual agents going to and from her office.

She reached the end of the hall and stood before a massive iron door, its surface marred with scratches and rust. Above it, another sign stared back at her: *Labor Penitentiary—No Magic Beyond This Point.* Morvina's sour lips curled in disdain as she heaved the door open and saw the long, winding staircase descending into depths below.

The steps were narrow and uneven, made of ancient stone that had grown brittle and crumbly over centuries of neglect. The wall, lined with jagged rocks, provided little comfort, as the other side of the staircase was open, offering an unwelcome view into the abyss. One misstep, and she would plummet into the chasm.

Morvina began her descent, muttering a string of curse words under her breath. Her high heels made the journey perilous, each step requiring precise placement to avoid slipping. She could feel the edges of the steps crumbling slightly under her weight, sending tiny pebbles skittering into the void.

Minutes turned into hours as she continued downward, gripping the files tightly to her chest. The torches mounted sporadically along the wall did little to illuminate the path, and most have burned out from the day's use, waiting to be lit again by hand.

Her feet ached and her skinny legs burned with the effort of maintaining balance on the unforgiving steps.

 More curse words.

As she descended farther, evidence of the work prison began to reach her—the rhythmic pounding of hammer against stone, mixed with the unpleasant stench of sweat and sulfur.

Tiny specks of light below eventually turned into roaring fires as Morvina reached the bottom of the staircase. She paused to catch her breath, dusting off her black pencil skirt, and surveyed her surroundings.

Demons of all backgrounds were doing an array of impossible jobs. In one corner, a group of prisoners, their bodies gaunt from relentless labor, were pounding massive stone blocks. The objective was to create a deeper staircase, a task that seemed both endless and pointless.

Nearby, another group carried large stones from one side of the encampment to the other, and back again. The stones were heavy and jagged, cutting into their hands and shoulders with each step. Every trip was a grueling test of endurance. As soon as they placed a stone down, they immediately picked it up and began the journey again. Morvina observed with a sour face, but was genuinely satisfied seeing the strict enforcement of infernal punishment.

Off to the side, sat a small office desk, starkly out of place. Sprawled among the disheveled papers and half-burned candles, a man was slumped over, asleep and snoring loudly. The noise of the prison seemed to have no effect on his slumber. Morvina approached him, her heels echoing sharply across the uneven, rocky ground. The demons around her didn't dare look at her, and remained completely consumed by their work.

Her eyes narrowed as she observed the sleeping man, His face was buried in the crook of his arm, his breath occasionally interrupted by a loud snore. His uniform marked him as a security guard, although it was clear he took his duties less seriously than he should, and as a demon, it was clear that he slept from boredom rather than necessity.

Finally, she slammed the files down with a resounding thud that jolted him awake. He jerked upright, eyes wide with panic as he took in the sight of Morvina standing before him.

"Morvina… I didn't see you there."

"Save it, Bellamy," she snapped. Morvina pointed a skinny finger down at the top file lying on Bellamy's desk. "I want him." Her tone was icy and to the point.

Bellamy glanced at the file, curiously. He read the name and shifted his eyes to the group of prisoners aimlessly pounding rocks. His brow furrowed in confusion as he looked back at her. "You want Ironfist? What for?"

Morvina leaned over the desk, pressing her bony knuckles into the surface, clearly annoyed by his audacity to question her. "That's none of your concern, now go *fetch* him." She straightened up, crossing her arms. "He's coming with me."

Bellamy sat up, nervously, attempting to exert his authority as a guard. "You know I can't let you do that, Morvina," he said, his voice shaking.

Morvina raised her eyebrows, her mind working swiftly to concoct a convincing lie. Her sour demeanor added weight to her words, making them believable. "I was sent under direct orders from *Soren*," she declared, her voice dripping with power. She leaned in closer, narrowing her pulled-back eyes. "I've seen your file, Bellamy. I really don't think you want me to share how you've been neglecting your duties down here—falling asleep, unlit torches..."

Bellamy's eyes widened at the mention of Soren, his face paling with fear. He stood up quickly, causing his chair to scrape loudly against the stone floor. "That won't be necessary," he stammered.

He looked over at the group of prisoners, his gaze settling on a hulking figure among them. With his newfound authority, he placed two fingers in his mouth and whistled loudly. The piercing sound cut through the groans and hammering. "Ironfist! You have a visitor!"

A hush fell over the prisoners at the sound of Ironfist's name, followed by numerous clanks as several of them dropped their tools and stones to watch, curiously. Ironfist stood up, pulling his muscular arm up to wipe his forehead.

He dropped his arms to his side and looked at his visitor, his sweaty brow furrowed. Bellamy, still nervously glancing at Morvina, motioned for him to come forward.

"So, his file says he managed to break the *No Magic* enforcement down here?" Morvina asked, eyeing the figure walking toward them.

"Yep. Killed the last guard as soon as he got here. That's how he got those." Bellamy was pointing at the two iron boxes that encased the demon's hands. While the other prisoners used giant sledgehammers to chip away at the unyielding stone, Ironfist used his own hands, which were imprisoned within the iron cages, earning him his nickname. He walked with a bow-legged gait, giving him a slow, exaggerated swagger. His arms were puffed out to the side, holding up the heavy, pitted cages.

As he approached the two, an overpowering stench of sweat and grime emanated from him. Morvina's face contorted even further in disgust. She cleared her throat, trying to hold a conversation through the odor. "I'm Mor..."

"I know who you are," Ironfist interrupted. "What do ya want?"

Morvina narrowed her eyes at his tone, but pressed on. "I have something to discuss with you. A *business* opportunity."

"Not interested in any business." Spit flew from his mouth, nearly hitting Morvina. She stepped back quickly, taking a moment to steady herself, and readjusted her skirt.

"This is a unique opportunity... *Mordac*, is it?" she asked, knowingly, picking up his file from Bellamy's desk.

"Not Mordac, anymore," he spat, holding his cages up in display.

"Yes, well, how would you like to *lose* those?"

Ironfist looked at her in surprise, raising a sweaty eyebrow. "I'm listening."

Morvina stepped back again, avoiding his spit, which was running down his chin. "So here's the deal—I'm working on a project... a *promotion* of sorts." Morvina paused, realizing Bellamy was listening. "Don't you have somewhere else to be?"

"Sorry..." Bellamy jumped and scurried away, pretending to tidy the mound of papers on his desk.

"So in order to get this promotion, I need a few tasks completed." She looked down at the second file next to her, curling her lip. "Jobs that another demon *failed* to do. This is a highly-secretive project, and I don't trust our agents to get it done. If I succeed, Soren will be working for *me,* if he's lucky." Bellamy's eyes widened as he struggled to listen.

"So what's in it for me?" Ironfist asked, suspiciously.

"Freedom."

A loud chatter arose from the prisoners at the word. Some stood wide-eyed in disbelief, while others nudged elbows and whispered amongst themselves, excited about the prospect of getting out of their oppressive atmosphere.

"Perhaps we should continue our conversation in private? Upstairs. If you're interested, that is."

"You gonna get rid of these?" Ironfist glanced down at his hands and then narrowed his eyes at her in hesitation.

"If you agree to my terms."

"Fine," Ironfist spat, then grumbled under his breath.

Morvina avoided his spit once more and grabbed the two files from Bellamy's desk, who was aimlessly shoveling papers around and avoiding eye contact. "Shouldn't they be working?" she asked him, coldly.

"Right!" He jumped at her words, whistling loudly once more. "Back to work! No more breaks!" The chatter died down as the prisoners reluctantly heaved their giant sledge-hammers over their shoulders and returned to work. The rhythmic pounding of stone and the groans of demons lifting jagged rocks filled the camp again as Morvina and Ironfist made their way to the staircase. Deciding she couldn't bear the stench any longer, Morvina insisted on going first.

As they began their ascent, the narrow, crumbling steps protested under Ironfist's massive weight. Each step he took caused fragile stone to crack and shift, sending shards tumbling onto the workers below. Morvina glanced back occasionally, her sour expression deepening as she watched him struggle up the stairs. She could hear his heavy breathing, and the sound of metal on stone as the iron cages scraped the wall.

She quickened her pace, eager to distance herself from the unsettling noises, and the spit that was now oozing from his mouth. The climb to the top took several hours longer than expected. As Morvina reached the top, she paused to catch her breath and narrowed her eyes on Ironfist, who was still climbing.

Centuries of pounding stone had built his muscles into unyielding slabs of strength, yet nothing could prepare him for the sheer exertion of heaving his weight up the spiraling staircase. His heavy breaths turned into ragged gasps as he finally reached the top, wiping the sweat pouring from his brow.

"Quickly, before we're seen." Morvina led the way down the dimly-lit corridor. After several turns, they arrived in a narrow hallway lined with small, dark offices. A small, tattered sign hung crookedly above the first door, barely legible in the flickering light: *Overseer Of Infernal Agents.*

"This your office?" Ironfist asked, squinting to read the tiny words.

"Not for long, if things go well." Morvina unlocked the door and ushered him inside. She cast a quick, careful glance throughout the hallway to ensure they were alone, then locked the door behind them. Her office was a cramped, dismal space, providing barely enough room for them to move around the rusted furniture. Boxes were stacked haphazardly, with documents spilling from them onto the floor. The walls were covered with faded, peeling tapestry, barely visible in the weak candlelight. She wasted no time getting to the point. She stood by a small desk in the center of the dark office, and placed the two files down, opening the top one.

"Mordac... no last name, goes by *Ironfist*. Sentenced to eternity in the Labor Department. Found guilty of stealing souls meant to be turned in and..." She paused as confusion and disgust crossed her face. "*consuming* them?"

"So what's it to you? We're here to talk about my freedom."

"Yes, well, we'll see how that goes. Finneas Ignautus was the demon originally assigned to these jobs. After not following orders, he got himself expelled. Because of him, our department has missed out on several thousand souls, just in the last century. *One* who is of the utmost importance to me. That's where you come in."

"How's that?"

"That's another *sensitive* process that requires bending a few rules. Altering files. In order to go undetected, I can only alter one assignment at a time, changing it from his assignment, to yours. Once you arrive at the past location, it will be like he was never there. You collect the souls according to the directions I give you, bring them to me, then we move onto the next assignment. Succeeding where Soren failed will get me the promotion I *deserve*. He should have never hired that half-wit demon, Finneas, in the first place."

"And how am I supposed to go back to the past? Demons can't do that," he asked, suspiciously.

"You can if you have *this*." Morvina opened Finn's file and pulled out a dainty, silver bracelet, its chain broken.

Ironfist tilted his head, squinting to read the words engraved on the front. "What's a *Letti*?"

"Her name is Scarlett. This belonged to her and it apparently fell here when Soren went to their little home, failing to bring her soul back, of course. He used his magic to turn it into some sort of tool in case he wanted one of our agents to be able to check up on them again. Well the assignment has been scrubbed—she's of no use to anyone... *now.* I've been *waiting* for the day when I can finally take her away from Finneas."

"Alright, where is she?" Ironfist straightened up, ready to begin.

"No, not yet. She comes last. We need as many souls as we can get, first. I need you to start here." She grabbed the top paper from Finn's file and passed her hand over it. *Finneas* was erased from the top of the page and replaced with *Mordac.* "Follow these directions carefully so we remain undetected, and bring the souls to me, *without* eating them." Morvina raised her pulled-back eyebrow to emphasize her instructions.

Ironfist let out a groan, setting his iron cages down on top of Morvina's desk. "I think I ought to keep *something* for myself. As a bonus, you know, for keeping quiet about all this. Say... twenty percent."

"Ten. I think your freedom is worth that—unless you prefer prison, of course."

"Alright, alright. Ten. You gonna take these off now?"

Morvina pursed her lips and passed her hand over the desk, causing the locked cages to snap open and disappear. Ironfist held up his hands, turning them over to admire the calloused palms, and scarred skin. He flexed his fingers slowly, watching in awe as they responded to his command, no longer shackled.

"Welcome back, Mordac," Morvina said with a sinister grin. "Your hands are free, and soon you will be too, if you cooperate. Now let's see this magic that got you into trouble. It may come in handy."

Mordac stood back, glancing at the boxes and grimy bookshelves that filled the tiny, dark room, and eyed the desk in the center once more. He raised his palm toward it, and electricity began to crackle and glow on his skin. Morvina's eyes widened, and she grabbed the files just in time as a bolt of lightning shot from his hand, instantly turning the desk into dust.

"Yes, that's perfect," Morvina smiled, unphased by her destroyed furniture. "If anyone gets in your way, *destroy them.* And most importantly, if anything goes wrong with the plan, leave immediately and go *here.*" She handed Mordac a small card with a photo of a green door, apartment number 111. He put the card in his pocket, along with the silver bracelet.

"No matter what," she added, "bring her to me *alive.*"

# CHAPTER TEN

## TRUTH

"Alright, we can talk. Is something wrong?" Finn inquired, perplexed by the atmosphere in the room.

Owlen's voice was steady, but his wide eyes carried concern that he couldn't hide from Finn. "I just want to catch up, *alone.* That's all." He cleared his throat and quickly glanced at Scarlett who still clung to Finn's waist. She understood their need for privacy after Owlen's absence, so she didn't question it. She squeezed Finn tightly once more and rested her chin on his chest, looking up at him, her eyes studying his face before excusing herself.

"I love you." Her words were just as much of a reassurance for her as they were a sign of affection for him. Guilt was making its way from her stomach to her face, and she blinked quickly to avoid any tears.

"Well, I love you, too." Finn was slightly surprised as he kissed her forehead. "We'll be out in a bit."

As Scarlett wandered outside, she could hear their voices clearly from inside the cottage. She tried to distance herself, but each word still found her, effortlessly. *Stupid enhanced hearing,* she thought, walking away more quickly now. She stopped for a moment to see if she had gone far enough, but although she could no longer hear their conversation, Owlen's words echoed in her mind, reading that poem with his soft, gentle voice.

Scarlett let out a loud, heavy sigh, covering her ears with her hands and closing her eyes tightly. In her mind she could see Finn, his beautiful, crimson eyes looking at her tenderly. She could never intentionally bring pain to those eyes, yet betrayal began to loom in her thoughts. A deep, inexplicable bond formed between her and Owlen during their time together. She was drawn to him in a way that unsettled her, and still, Finn's eyes looked at her with nothing but love. This only made the gnawing guilt fall to her stomach once more.

Scarlett dropped her hands to her side, giving them a shake. She focused on the gentle rustling of the leaves in the breeze, the vibrant colors of the flowers, and the soothing sound of the afternoon songbirds. Anything to calm her racing thoughts. Her steps were slow and contemplative as she made her way along the path that Finn had created to heal their land. Beautiful flowers lined the way, carefully placed there by her demon's unwavering love. She would never do anything to jeopardize that love, she tried to reassure herself again.

As she walked, her internal struggle was interrupted by something odd at her feet. She noticed its stark contrast to the colorful blooms surrounding it. There, nestled between flower stems, was a single, black feather. Scarlett kneeled down, scooping it up gently, observing its fragile state. The shaft was broken in half, being held together by a delicate thread. The end was charred and brittle, like a candle wick that had long been extinguished. Her breath caught in her throat, and her mouth fell open with sudden realization.

It was Finn's feather.

Scarlett stood up, her eyes quickly scanning the path for more feathers, but after a thorough search, this remained the only one. A defeated sigh escaped her lips as she sat down on the path. Tears were forming in her amethyst eyes as she clutched the damaged feather. Visions of Soren brutally ripping Finn's wings from his body came rushing back to her. Watching helplessly in horror as they were crushed into pieces, feathers floating down into the seething lava that divided their world. It was a painful reminder of his selfless sacrifice for her, and it made the guilt she felt about Owlen claw at her insides.

She stroked the broken feather in her palm, wishing more than anything that she could give back what was taken, and make Finn whole again. She stared off, imagining his beautiful wings unfurled around her, just as they were when he pulled her from the flames. As her fingers traced the surface, the feather suddenly felt different beneath her touch, and she glanced down, curiously. Her eyes widened in disbelief at what she saw—it was no longer broken in half. The charred tips were mended, returning the feather to its dark, flawless glory, the ends now glowing with beautiful embers, just as she remembered.

Scarlett's heart raced in her chest as she studied the repaired feather. Was this Finn's lingering magic, or had she done this herself? The idea of having such power was tantalizing, and the gnawing guilt in her stomach shifted to excitement, but her doubts quickly brought her back to reality. *What if this was a fluke? A one-time thing, maybe?* Disappointment began to set in at the thought.

Taking a deep breath, Scarlett decided to experiment. With a wince, she snapped the feather between her fingers, breaking it in half. Smoke wisped from the frayed tips, and for a moment, the feather lay broken in her palm. With a gentle touch, she glided her fingers over the fragments, and just as before, the feather became seamlessly whole.

She let out a sigh of relief, realizing that she had been holding her breath. *It could still just be magic in the feather,* she thought, calming her excitement. She placed it gently in her lap and searched her surroundings. White flowers resembling daisies were gathered around her legs, their blooms, like curious little faces, poked in her direction. Scarlett reached for one, being careful not to pull it from the ground. She admired its beauty for a moment, with a contemplative expression. "I'm sorry about this," she whispered, before holding her breath once more, and she carefully tore the delicate petals in half, leaving the mutilated bloom lifeless in her hand.

As her fingertips grazed the broken pieces, she gently rested the tip of the stem on the small heap in her palm. She focused on healing, just as she had done with the feather. To her astonishment, the petals gradually knit themselves together, finding their place on the stem. The little flower peered up at her as if nothing had happened. A triumphant smile crossed Scarlett's face as she let out her breath in relief once more.

She looked down at her hands. They seemed ordinary, but they now held an extraordinary ability—the power to mend what is broken, just as her demon could. A plan was forming in her mind, and she would need Owlen's help... *if* she could hold herself together. *Whatever happened earlier can't happen again*, she thought. She immediately felt a pang of sadness at the thought, but she shook her head, closing her eyes tightly as if willing the feeling to disappear. Owlen was her *friend*. That's it. Thinking of him as anything else felt like a betrayal.

She pictured Finn, his crimson eyes looking into hers. She could feel the warmth of his skin as he reached for her face. His veins formed a delicate pattern across the back of his hand and up his forearm, which made her knees buckle. Her breath quickened as she felt his other hand press on the small of her back, pulling her in closer so their bodies were touching. Her hand followed the hard muscles of his chest up to the back of his neck, where she pulled him down toward her, eager to meet his lips.

"Trust me, just give it time." Finn's voice pulled Scarlett from her daydream, and she looked up to see the two emerging from the cottage. She stood up and quickly shoved the feather into her pocket, snapping it again to conceal its glow.

She sensed something different as she approached Finn and Owlen, like a shift in their dynamic. It must have done them both some good to finally spend time together, but she couldn't help but wonder what they discussed. Scarlett was beginning to wish she hadn't tried so hard to drown out their conversation. The brief silence that lingered between the three of them brought knots to her stomach. Had Owlen told Finn about her foolish behavior earlier? What did *just give it time* mean? Were they planning something?

Finn took the lead, breaking the silence, with a mischievous glint in his eyes. "So, we've decided it's time for Owlen to start joining us out here, if that's okay with you. At night, I mean. No more being cooped up by himself." Owlen, standing nervously beside Finn, stole a quick glance at Scarlett. His heart quickened as he anxiously gauged her reaction. The newfound connection between them had stirred something unspoken, and he couldn't help but wonder how she felt about the new arrangement.

Scarlett felt the weight of their gazes as they awaited her response. Doing her best to remain casual, she replied. "Sure, that's fine." Her nonchalant tone masked the flutter she felt on the inside—a precautionary measure to avoid revealing too much.

Finn, with a new, keen perception of the situation, caught the nuance in Scarlett's response. His eyes flickered between the two, recognizing the unspoken swirl of emotions. He nudged Owlen, playfully. "Looks like we got the approval, angel. Nightly garden meetings, it is. Or should we call them *stream meetings*? No, that sounds weird."

Owlen, though visibly relieved, maintained an air of uncertainty. "If that's what you both want," he added, still searching Scarlett's expression for any sign of discomfort.

"Of course it is. You're always welcome, remember?" Scarlett gave him a genuine smile.

Owlen smiled in return, shifting his gaze away quickly to avoid blushing. By then, the sun had dipped below the horizon. He looked around them, noticing the subtle shift of night through the garden. As they made their way under the sprawling tree, flower buds were closing up for their nap, and birds had stopped singing as they snuggled into their nests for the night. The Moon made the stream glisten like silvery silk before them, and the Earth's familiar reflection was playing on the water's surface.

"It really is beautiful at night, isn't it? It's been ages since I've enjoyed the darkness." He glanced at the others to see if they shared his amazement, but they were already settled in the grass. Finn was sitting with his legs criss-crossed, gliding his strong fingers gently through Scarlett's long brown hair. Her eyes were closed, not out of sleepiness, but pure contentment.

Owlen suddenly felt like he was imposing on a private moment, and the familiar sense of being an outsider found him again. He looked around for an appropriate place to sit, wondering if he should have instead left them alone.

"Angel, what are you doing? Sit down." Finn patted the ground next to them.

Scarlett looked up and saw the uncertainty in his blue eyes, and visions began to flood her mind. Her head rested on Owlen's lap, his gentle hands combing through her hair, carefully returning each strand to its place. His beautiful eyes studied her features like words on a page, sliding his hand delicately down her arm, and intertwining his fingers with hers...

"Isn't it?" Finn's voice pulled her back to them, and she was jolted from her thoughts.

"Sorry, what?" Scarlett's cheeks turned pink when she realized they were both seated next to her now, awaiting her response.

"I said this is going to be interesting isn't it? The three of us out here with nothing to do—hanging out, chatting." Finn was looking back and forth between his friends. Scarlett looked down in embarrassment for losing control of her thoughts again, while Owlen shrugged nervously, hoping not to be put on the spot with conversation. Finn rolled his eyes and gave him a slight nudge, tilting his head toward Scarlett, encouraging Owlen to speak.

"Uh… s-so Scarlett," Owlen stuttered, searching for something to fill the awkward silence. "I, uh, never really got to hear how things were for you, before you came here."

Finn's eyes widened. This was not what he meant by *chatting*. The last thing he wanted was Scarlett reminiscing about another life, as selfish as that may be. "Angel," he chuckled through his worry, "she doesn't want to go into all that. Let's talk about something else."

"No, it's okay." Scarlett sat up, happy to concentrate her thoughts onto another topic. "I don't mind. What do you want to know?"

Owlen, slightly pleased with himself, continued. "Well, let's see. Did you have a job? I've always found motal jobs so fascinating."

Scarlett chuckled. "It definitely wasn't fascinating, but yes, I had a job. I was a waitress at *Off The Bone.*"

The look on Owlen's face told her that she should probably elaborate. "It's a restaurant that serves ribs and wings."

The look again.

"Just something that people like to eat," she explained, trying not to laugh.

"That sounds lovely, doesn't it?" Owlen glanced at Finn, seeking his approval as the conversation began to flow, but Finn was lost in his own thoughts, staring off into the darkness.

"Was there anyone special you left behind, like a m-mate?" He attempted to sound casual, but he couldn't hide the stammer in his voice at the thought of her dating, and he smiled nervously.  He noticed Finn shifting uncomfortably out of the corner of his eye, and his smile faded.

"No, no boyfriend," Scarlett smiled. "Not since high-school. I *was* dating someone for a while, but we decided to break up before graduation. He was going out of state to play college football, so it just seemed like the best thing to do."

"College?" Owlen's eyes lit up. "That sounds so exciting! You're very lucky to have experienced that." But his expression changed when saw Scarlett staring solemnly at the ground.

"I didn't."

"Oh..." Heat rose into Owlen's face, and he shifted nervously. "Of course. I'm so sorry. I didn't realize..."

"It's okay," Scarlett shrugged, her eyes remaining fixed at her feet. "Before my parents died, a lot of businesses were closing, and my dad was let go from his job. He lost their health insurance, life insurance, everything. They got sick so quickly, he didn't even have enough time to apply for assistance or unemployment benefits, so college wasn't an option for me anymore. I used the money I had saved for school to pay for their funeral expenses." A tear landed on the grass beneath her before Scarlett realized she was crying.

Owlen gave her some time to reflect in the quiet night. *Her life was so tragic*, he thought to himself. *Full of human experiences, as it should be, but tragic.* He glanced over at Finn, and saw him wipe a tear with his shoulder, still shrouded in silence. He didn't need to speak. Owlen could see exactly what he was thinking and feeling. Eyes closed, he used his powers to immerse himself within Finn's mind.

Emotions swirled around him like a dark, stormy cyclone, and he worked quickly to pull the deepest ones from the chaos, holding them gently as though they were one of his delicate flowers. Owlen watched as the love that Finn felt for his two soulmates calmed the storm within his mind over and over again. He felt grounded, protective, and drawn toward them with a fierce intensity that the cyclone couldn't match. It was a relief to see that Finn felt this way. Owlen would never dare ask. But just as the storm would calm, doubt and grief returned in a vicious cycle.

Burning questions plagued the corners of his mind. *Would Scarlett be happier without me? What if Owlen couldn't save her? If she gets her powers, will she want to leave us?* Owlen opened his eyes, returning back to his friends. He could spend the entire night within Finn's mind if he wanted to, knowing when he returned, only a moment would have passed. A blink. He reached over, squeezing Finn's elbow, causing him to startle. He was used to Owlen peering into his emotions, so it was no surprise when Finn gave him a slight, knowing grin in return, most likely from embarrassment.

Owlen, sensing a need for a change in tone, broke the silence. "Well, enough about the past. What else shall we discuss? Let's see..." He tapped his fingertips together for a moment, and to his relief, Scarlett spoke.

"So, Owlen, I was thinking we could pick up where we left off... you teaching me about the different flowers, I mean." She did her best to sound nonchalant again. She did love spending time with Owlen. She loved listening to him go on endlessly about something he was so passionate about, but truthfully, she was dying to show him her powers, and hopefully get his advice on how she was planning on using them. But one step at a time. She needed to get him alone. "If it's okay with Finn." He snapped from his thoughts and turned to meet her eyes at the sound of his name. "You've barely talked all night. Are you alright?" she asked, nudging him.

Finn realized how absorbed in his own thoughts he had become, and made an effort to be present in the conversation. He wrapped his arms around Scarlett, pulling her toward him with a reassuring smile. "Of course, just listening. But please, go on without me. If I have to sit through angel droning on about his plants one more time, it'll be the first time I fall asleep."

Owlen, who was practically holding his breath waiting for a response, let out a gasp of excitement. "Oh thank you! Well, this will be fun, won't it? When should we start? How about in the morning? Oh I can't wait! You really are missing out, Finn."

Finn rolled his eyes and smirked at Owlen's excitement. "You're like a Golden Retriever, you know that?"

Scarlett smiled at the both of them as they carried on, playfully. Owlen was right—enough about the past. Even with everything that happened to bring her to this moment, she had never felt happier or more content than she felt with both of them. At the same time, she could feel a shift, a change. An unsettling feeling that something was coming. Revealing her powers could only bring them all closer. She would no longer feel like the boring human who came here wrapped in Finn's wings... so why did an uneasy feeling still linger?

As the world around them began to wake up with the morning's rays, the three stood up, eager to leave this night behind them. Owlen sighed, looking down at his clothes. His usually-pristine ensemble was now wrinkled, with bits of dirt and grass on his backside. He cleared his throat, and with a slight wave of his hand, his clothes were now clean and perfectly pressed.

Finn chuckled and shook his head. "So that's how you crawl around all day talking to plants without a speck of dirt on you. Bravo."

Owlen blushed slightly and looked down at where he had been sitting. "I know I'm the new one here, but may I please make a suggestion?"

"Sure," Scarlett and Finn both agreed.

"Would it be too much trouble to spend some nights inside? Or at least not on the ground?"

"No trouble at all, angel. Of course, we'd have to make it a little more comfortable for all of us. You know, I was thinking of making some adjustments to the cottage anyway." Finn rubbed his hands together and smiled. A look of panic crossed Owlens face, but before he could speak,

Finn raised his hand. "Don't worry, angel, I'll behave. Nothing crazy, I promise. Run along, now."

Owlen glanced at the cottage, nervously, and then ushered Scarlett toward the path. She wrapped her arms around Finn's waist, kissing him before following Owlen.

Scarlett kept glancing behind her as they walked along the path, only half-listening as Owlen carried on excitedly about propagation. After one more careful look toward the cottage, Finn was finally out of sight. "So we can collect some samples today, and I can show you..."

Scarlett put her hands up, cutting Owlen off mid-sentence. "Owlen, I'm so sorry but I need to show you something."

Owlen's interest was piqued as he watched Scarlett reach into her pocket and pull out the broken feather. His eyes widened with realization as he gasped. "Oh my! Is that...?"

"His," Scarlett confirmed. "I found it yesterday. I looked around, but this is the only one I saw."

Owlen's expression turned solemn as he studied the feather in her hand, and Scarlett touched his arm gently to comfort him. "But watch, this is what I wanted to show you." She focused on the feather in her palm and took a deep breath as she passed her other hand over it. Just as before, the feather was now whole, embers smoldering at the tips.

"Goodness gracious!" Owlen put a hand to his mouth as he gasped. "You have powers!"

"I do," Scarlett smiled. It was a relief to finally share her secret with him. "At least, I *think* I do. This is all I can do for now. That's why I need your help."

"Of course! Anything you need, my dear. Oh, this is so exciting!" His blue eyes glistened as he admired the familiar embers. "What did you have in mind?"

Scarlett thought to herself for a moment, trying to figure out how to divulge her plan without sounding silly. Owlen would never make her feel silly, though. He was always supportive, always eager to help. He really was perfect in every way. "I want to give him wings."

"Oh!" Owlen put his hand on his chest. At first, a look of astonishment crossed his face, and after a moment he met her eyes with genuine gratitude. "I'm sure you already know how much that would mean to me. If I were able to do it myself, well..." He blinked quickly and looked away before his tears had a chance to fall.

"I know," Scarlett nodded. "I'm just worried that I'll try and it won't work. I'd feel horrible if I got his hopes up for nothing. I want to get it *absolutely* right, you know?"

Owlen dried his eyes and turned toward her again. "It seems that you have already been practicing. That's definitely a start. What you've learned so far is truly remarkable," he smiled, taking her hand into his. She found it hard to look into his eyes. *Not now. Stay focused,* she thought to herself. "So, do you think you can help me, then?"

"Yes, of course!" Owlen smiled. "We can start now if you'd like. Shall we sit?" He looked at the ground around him and remembered his dirty pants from earlier. "This won't do. Let's have a seat at the table instead." Owlen held out his elbow and guided Scarlett farther up the path to the familiar picnic table surrounded by purple flowers.

They both took their places, and Owlen clasped his hands together for a moment, thinking. "You've done very well so far. Healing something that is broken is an extraordinary power to have. Unfortunately, Finn's wings aren't broken, they are... *non-existent.*"

Scarlett nodded, sadly.

"So now," Owlen continued, "we must focus on creating something from nothing, and it's all about the mind." Owlen passed his hand over the space in front of him, and a beautiful, purple butterfly appeared on the table. He lowered his hand, where it jumped happily to his finger, stretched its wings a few times, and then fluttered away.

"I definitely want to learn how to do that! You make it look so easy." Scarlett had seen Owlen use his magic many times, but now that his powers were also within her reach, she was amazed all over again.

"It will become easier for you, my dear. We'll start small. But I promise you, butterfly wings, or demon wings, it all works the same. So don't let size discourage you."

Scarlett let out a sigh of relief. As doubt was creeping in, making her question her abilities, Owlen was there, as always, to offer his unwavering support. Scarlett met his gentle eyes, and he grinned, nervously directing his attention to his suddenly anxious hands. "So... uh... like I said, no matter what you are trying to create, it's all about the m..."

Owlens words began to fade and Scarlett realized that she hadn't been listening, and was, instead, staring at his lips. It was the poem all over again, and she tried to bring herself back quickly before Owlen would notice.

*Focus... focus.*

Owlen did, in fact, notice a furrowed expression on Scarlett's face that resembled pain, and he immediately reached for her hand. "My goodness, are you alright?"

Scarlett's cheeks flushed as she was embarrassingly snapped back to reality. "I'm fine," she muttered. "I just need to focus more, I guess." She thought of Finn and the familiar pang of guilt found her stomach again. *He deserves so much more than this*, she thought. *I need to stop. I wish I could stop. Why can't that be as easy as fixing a feather?* Finn deserved to be whole again, and the only way that could happen is with Owlen's help. "Can we please start over? I'm sorry."

"Of course, my dear." A look of confusion crossed Owlen's face, but he offered another encouraging smile. "No need to apologize. Now as I was saying, it's all about the mind. I want you to give it a try. Start with something small if you'd like. Think of an object, and when it's in your mind, make it appear in front of you using the same powers you used to heal the feather."

Sacrlett nodded, her eyes fixed on the table in front of her. She concentrated, extending her hand toward the blank space. After a moment, her hand began to tremble slightly, and with a frustrated huff, she dropped it to the table.

"Take a deep breath, my dear," Owlen coached, his voice still soothing. "Find the stillness within you. Let go of the frustration and try again."

Scarlett closed her eyes, drawing in a deep breath and slowly exhaling. Her mind cleared and she raised her palm again. She waited longer this time, doing her best to stay focused. When she opened her eyes, the space in front of her remained empty. "It's not working," she muttered, disappointment and worry evident in her voice."

"That's alright, my dear" Owlen reassured her. He placed his hands on hers. His gentle demeanor provided a much-needed anchor in the sea of doubt that was forming. "Let's try a different approach. I know you want this to work so badly that it's possible you are wishing for it. Now, it's very important not to *wish* for something. You are essentially creating reality. Wishing takes the power out of your hands. Does that make sense?"

"I think so."

"Instead of wishing or hoping, you must imagine something as though it already exists in front of you. You're already very capable of that. When you repaired that feather, you didn't *wish* for it to repair itself, you pictured it whole in your mind, as though it were never broken, correct?"

"Actually, yes!" Scarlett smiled. "I didn't even realize."

"When you become more accustomed to your powers, creating something will happen instantaneously. However, behind the scenes, all of your senses will be working together to achieve that.

"So if we take Finn's wings, for example, you must picture them as though they are already right in front of you. How do they look? Imagine their beauty beneath the moonlight. Imagine how they feel while you glide your fingers over them as he stands before you."

"I think I can do that. I hope so, anyway. I really have only one shot at this. I don't think he would want me to keep trying if it doesn't work."

"Finn can definitely be stubborn," he chuckled. "But no worries, my dear. I'm absolutely certain you can do this."

Scarlett definitely appreciated his confidence in her. She looked down at the space in front of her, before closing her eyes. She took a moment, allowing her senses to work together, and then slowly passed her hand over the table. When she opened her eyes, Owlen was looking down in front of her, gleaming. She gasped as a beautiful purple butterfly looked up at her, stretched its wings, and then fluttered away, joining its mate among the flowers surrounding them.

"I knew you could do it! Oh!" Owlen clutched his chest once more and could barely contain his excitement. "You really are a natural at this. I'm so proud!"

"Thank you, Owlen. I really couldn't have done it without you." She passed her hand across the table again and a purple rose appeared before her. She smiled as she picked it up and examined it, before handing it to Owlen. "Really, thank you for everything."

Owlen graciously accepted the rose, and blushed. "I was happy to do it. You had it in you all along, you just needed a little guidance. I'm so pleased that our friend may be himself once more." He smelled the rose for a moment before rising from his seat. "Shall we walk back now? To be honest, I'm a bit nervous leaving Finn to look after the cottage. There's no telling what he has done."

Scarlett laughed and got up from her seat. Butterflies started forming in her stomach as she went over her plan in her head, and soon, butterflies turned to gnawing knots of doubt. Owlen placed her hand on his elbow, and as they began walking, her nerves calmed. "Thanks," she said, giving him a genuine smile.

The two of them approached the cottage, which was seemingly normal from the outside. Owlen let out a small sigh of relief, but braced himself as he slowly opened the door. His eyes widened as he looked around the living room. Finn was relaxing on a giant, leather sofa that wrapped around two of the walls. His hands were behind his head and he grinned at the both of them "Now *this* is better, don't you think?" His legs were stretched out and near his feet was a beautiful, stone fireplace with a crackling fire glowing inside.

"It's... um... a bit *warm* for a fire, isn't it?" Owlen wasn't sure how he felt about the changes.

"Don't worry, angel, it's purely aesthetic. Go on, touch it."

Owlen walked over and slowly lowered his hand toward the fireplace. "Well," he said, slightly impressed. "That really is something. Look at this Scarlett." Scarlett joined him and slowly placed her hands near the fireplace, and after a moment, she reached her hand inside the flames. Her mouth fell open in amazement.

"See?" Finn said with a smug grin. "Nothing to worry about. All your knick-knacks are still over there, next to your hoard of books. I just rearranged them a bit." Owlen let out another sigh at the sight of his belongings. "Anyway, this should suffice when *one* doesn't want to get *one's* precious clothes dirty."

"Thank you," Owlen gave Finn a genuine smile. "It really is lovely. This will do nicely." He glanced at Scarlett and gave her a slight, encouraging nod.

*It was time.*

# CHAPTER ELEVEN

## UNVEIL

Scarlett gave Owlen a small nod in return and took a deep breath. She extended her hand toward Finn, who gave her a puzzled look, pulling himself to his feet.

"What are you two being so weird about?" he asked, being playfully suspicious.

"I want to show you something," Scarlett replied, her voice shaking slightly as she tried to calm her nerves. "But I don't think there is enough room here, do you?" She eyed the massive couch, then gave Owlen a pleading look, hoping for some direction.

Owlen picked up on her cue and stood up quickly. "Perhaps outside would be best, then. You two go ahead, and I'll wait here."

Finn put his arm around Scarlett's shoulder, pressing his lips to her ear. "Got a surprise for me, eh?" His warm breath ignited a rush of goosebumps across her skin.

"Uh... y-yeah, sort of," she stuttered. "Are you sure you don't want to come with us?" she asked Owlen as they made their way to the door.

"I'm sure, my dear. But I'd love to hear all about it when you return." He gave her a proud smile, and as Finn walked outside, Owlen pulled Scarlett aside for a moment, whispering.

"Remember everything I told you. You can do this. It's all about the mind, so focus on your thoughts."

Scarlett gave him a nod.

"I'll watch from here, if you don't mind. I'd love to see it, but I wouldn't want to make Finn uncomfortable. I hope you understand."

"Yeah, that's true, especially if this doesn't work."

Owlen put his hand on Scarlett's shoulders, gently, pulling her from her doubts again. "It *will* work."

"Thanks again." She gave him a quick hug, and as she walked out the door, she looked back at him. "Wish me luck."

"Good luck, my dear." He gave her a genuine smile before closing the door. He knew very well that Scarlett didn't need luck. The magic was already inside of her. What she needed was the confidence to use it.

As he took his place by the window, Owlen could sense a shift—a change in the air, as if something were about to happen. Something extraordinary, he hoped. But he couldn't help but think of the last time he had this feeling—the day the sky turned black and their lives were forever changed. *It's going to be fine,* he thought to himself as he looked on at his friends.

The Moon and Earth hung high in the sky above them as Scarlett and Finn made their way to the stream. "So, can you tell me *now* what's going on?" Finn stood in front of her, grinning as he crossed his arms.

Scarlett remained serious, working hard to stay focused on her plan. "Can you kneel down? Please?" She gave a quick glance to Owlen, who was standing vigil in the window.

Finn gave her a curious look, and then did as she asked. Scarlett walked behind him, dragging her fingertips delicately along his collarbone, over his shoulder, and down his back, where she grasped the bottom of his shirt. She took a deep breath and began lifting it up, and as Finn realized she was attempting to remove it, he pulled the shirt off and tossed it to the ground.

"Well, I like where this is going so far," he said quietly. He stole a glance at her from the corner of his eye.

*Focus, focus.*

Scarlett kneeled down behind him, his back now exposed to her. She stared for a moment, taking in the beauty of his form. The reflection of the water rippling across his skin, the moonlight accentuating every muscle.

*Focus.*

She placed her fingers at the base of his neck and slowly traced her way to the prominent scars that disfigured him. She could feel Finn suddenly become tense, and she knew it was not from pain, but insecurity caused by his marred skin. Scarlett leaned in and whispered, reassuring him. "It's okay, trust me." Finn swallowed hard and closed his eyes tightly, but allowed her to continue.

Scarlett closed her eyes as well, Finn's form engraved in her mind. Her hands traced the air just above his skin, gliding them out and down to the ground as she imagined his beautiful feathers beneath her fingers. She pictured him standing before her, his unfurled wings spanning around them, just as they did when he brought her to Owlen. They were different than before, and possessed an otherworldly beauty that matched Finn's flawless features.

As she passed her hand over his back, Finn let out a gasp, and Scarlett caught herself from falling as he jumped to his feet. His eyes widened as he took in the sight of his wings, now stretched out behind him.

Tears fell freely as Owlen watched the transformation take place. He was pleasantly surprised to see the new wings that Scarlett had envisioned for Finn—far from the dark, smoldering ones that were ripped away. A lunar glow now surrounded him as each silvery feather rippled like moonlight in the stream.

Finn was speechless, his mind absorbing the moment. He reached out tentatively, running his fingers along the smooth surface of the feathers. He looked up to meet Scarlett's gaze, who sighed with relief as she admired the results. Finn's eyes were shining with unshed tears of gratitude. "I..." His voice choked with gratitude as he struggled for words. "Thank you."

Scarlett walked forward, wrapping her hands around his waist, his skin warm against her cheek. "You're welcome," she whispered. "It's the least I could do after everything, you know? And Owlen helped a lot."

Finn saw Owlen's figure standing in the glowing window of their cottage, and gave him a gracious wave. "So, your powers are pretty impressive already." He grinned as he lay down, gesturing for her to join him.

"I'm still figuring them out, but if doing this for you is all I'll ever be able to do, then it was worth it."

Finn pressed his lips to hers and flipped over, pulling her underneath him. As he leaned over her, his wings surrounded them, shielding them from the night.

As Owlen watched, his heart painfully clenched in his chest, and loneliness was once again nagging at him from within. The weight of his friends' connection was pressing on him, and he found it hard to breathe.

Owlen turned away from the window, unable to witness any more. As he began slowly pacing, awaiting their return, a stark realization struck him, and he felt suddenly ill. *He* was the shift. *He* was the change he felt in the air.

His vision blurred at the edges, and he staggered before lowering himself onto the couch, tightly clutching a nearby pillow to his chest. His head was spinning, sorting details in his mind. He was there to save Scarlett when she died, helped her to make Finn whole again—but what now? He was no longer needed.

Owlen was once again an outsider to the undeniable bond between Finn and Scarlett, and tears began to fall to the pillow he clung to. He heard footsteps approaching the door, and he stood up quickly, wiping his face. He knew what had to be done. He had made a heartbreaking resolution, and it was time to tell his friends.

Finn burst through the door, eager to show off his gift from Scarlett. "Just when you thought I couldn't get any more handsome, eh?"

Owlen forced a smile, hoping to mask the turmoil churning inside him. "They're just beautiful—they really suit you. And Scarlett, you did so well. I'm so proud of you." He tried to remain cheerful, despite the ache in his chest.

Finn walked toward Owlen with a confident swagger, and with a dramatic flourish, he spread his arms wide, giving Owlen a better look. "Ta-da! Feast your eyes, angel!" Scarlett laughed and wrapped her arms around him. With a thought,

Finn's wings were instantly concealed, and he pulled her into a kiss.

Owlen's heart twisted even further, and his smile faltered. He stood up straight, adjusting his clothes before taking a deep breath. His friends were still consumed in their embrace, so he cleared his throat before making his announcement.

"I suppose," he began nervously, causing his voice to go a little louder than anticipated, "now that things have returned to normal, it's time that I... move on." The words burned in his throat, and as Scarlett looked at him with confusion in her amethyst eyes, he found it difficult to stand.

"What do you mean *move on*? Are you leaving?" She laughed after hearing herself ask him such a ridiculous question. But as she saw him glance at Finn, the look of terror that washed over Owlen's face caused her to look up as well, and her mouth fell open. Finn was staring at Owlen, *seething*. His red eyes bore into him with an intensity that neither of them had ever seen before.

"Finn, please don't do this. You must have known I would have to leave eventually. I..."

"Scarlett, go outside." Finn didn't take his eyes off of Owlen, who was wiping beads of sweat from his forehead with a handkerchief from his pocket.

"What's going on?" Scarlett looked at both of them, waiting for an answer.

A deep rumbling growl left his throat as he spoke through his teeth, clenching his fists. "Outside. *Now.*"

Scarlett's eyes widened at his tone, but without further question, she walked past Owlen and went outside, shutting the door behind her. Anxiety was building in her stomach, and she calmed her breath so she could hear their conversation.

"What in the hell are you doing?" Finn's eyes were burning through him.

Owlen shifted uncomfortably at Finn's aggression. "I... I just think it's for the best," he stammered, his voice faltering.

"And I told you to give her more time!" Finn's voice rose to a dangerous pitch, and Scarlett jumped at the sound. He took a breath, controlling his rage. "You really think *leaving* is for the best?  Dammit, I thought you were smarter than that, angel."

Owlen recoiled slightly at Finn's words. "I can't do this anymore. You have to understand what I'm going through."

"And you think you'd survive? We share a soul now. You might as well be dead on your own."

"This is killing me either way, whether I stay or go. Please understand." Owlen's expression softened, his gaze pleading.

Anger wasn't working. Finn's heart was pounding as he searched his mind for the right words to say. Anything to make Owlen stay. In a last desperate attempt, he approached Owlen, forcing him to look into his crimson eyes. "What about *Luminara?* We made this place together, remember?

Look at everything you've done to it—making it into a home. You're willing to leave all of this behind?"

"Don't you understand? I made it for *you.*" Owlen's voice softened as he placed a hand on Finn's shoulder. "All of this was for you. I hoped that one day you would see it and want to return to me. Those alleys and sewers were no place for you. You deserved to be here, in the sunlight. Luminara is yours now."

Tears welled up in Finn's eyes as he turned away, realizing he had lost this battle. He slumped on the couch, burying his head in his hands.

"I won't leave without saying goodbye," Owlen added softly as he walked outside, leaving the door open behind him. Scarlett stared at him in shock, waiting for him to say something to her, but he walked past, unable to look at her.

"Owlen!" She called after him, but he continued walking on the path until he was out of sight.

Scarlett walked in to find Finn sobbing, his hands clenching his long hair, tightly. "You need to tell me what's going on." She stood over him, wanting to offer comfort, but demanded some needed answers first. What did he mean by *giving her more time*? She had heard him say that before. And Finn and Owlen sharing a soul? That's impossible.

Finn let out a scream of anguish as he grabbed a crystal vase from Owlen's shelf. He threw it toward the door, where it crashed against the wall in a deafening shatter. Splinters of glass scattered in all directions, but Scarlett kept her eyes on him, unaffected by his display of rage.

Finn wiped his eyes with the bottom of his shirt and looked up at her with a defeated gaze. "He's leaving us."

"I heard that, but *why?*"

Finn sat, looking contemplatively into the fire, his tear-stained face glowing as he tapped his fingertips together. "Let me ask you something," he said, holding his gaze on the flames. "Do you ever find yourself, I don't know, *drawn* to Owlen now? Like you have to be near him?"

Scarlett stared at him, frozen. Her mouth fell open slightly, but she was unable to speak. Her mind worked quickly, trying to form a response, but before she could speak, Finn continued. "Maybe you find yourself looking at him differently than before? Having feelings for him that go beyond friendship? Like something deeper is pulling you toward him?"

"I... I don't..." Scarlett stuttered as she lowered her head. How did he know? Was her behavior that obvious? A lump formed in her throat and she suddenly felt sick. As she raised her head, Finn was looking at her with knowing eyes, and she realized that truth was her only option. She nodded silently.

"Yeah?" Finn responded, not surprised by her answer. "Me too."

This jerked Scarlett from her thoughts. "*What?*"

"Well, I've been able to control it pretty well, but it's there. Same as you."

Scarlett shifted, stepping back slightly, visibly uncomfortable with this conversation. "So what are you saying? What does this have to do with Owlen leaving?"

Finn sat up, gentleness filling his crimson eyes, catching her attention. "You already knew it was Owlen who brought you back when you died, right?"

Scarlett nodded.

"Well, what you *don't* know, and what I didn't find out until recently, was *how.* I'm not going to pretend to know all the details, but somehow when I was taking your soul, he did too... because we were all holding hands, maybe. So when he saved you, it's because he still had a piece of your soul. We're lucky he's so smart and realized it in time. Whatever the reason is, we are *all* soulmates. Not just me and you."

Realization flooded through Scarlett, and things were beginning to make sense. Her purple eyes—a mix of blue and red. Every time her heart leapt. Every time she stared too long. Finn and Owlen were feeling the same way. "So why didn't either of you just tell me?"

"Because he's too *fucking* sensitive!" Finn raised his voice and stopped to take a calming breath. "He made me promise not to say anything until he found out the truth for himself. But that's the thing—he could look at you for two seconds and see every thought in your head, but he refuses to. He's too afraid to find out you don't feel the same way he and I do, I guess."

Finn stared off, his eyes carrying a defeated gaze. "He'll never make it out there, you know? He'll waste away without us.

And we have each other, but it'll never be the same without him."

Scarlett thought of their time without Owlen, after her change. Just mere days felt like an eternity. A void formed between her and Finn that only Owlen could fill. The thought of him leaving made it hard to breathe, and she could see the pain on Finn's face as well. "So what do we do?"

Finn reached out, grabbing her hand and gently pulling her toward him. "If you feel about him how I think you do, you need to show him. *Please.*" He tried to calm the desperation in his voice.

The familiar guilt settled in her stomach again and her eyes widened at the thought. "How can you be okay with that? It's... *deceitful.* I can't."

"Believe me, if it were any other man, I'd bury him *beneath* Hell myself." Anger seared through Finn, causing the flames to intensify and spark.

A solemn expression crossed Scarlett's face, and Finn's eyes softened as he squeezed her hand. "I promise I'd never ask you to do anything you don't want to do, and I'll never blame you if he leaves. But we're out of time, and he won't listen to me. So I'm begging you, if you feel the same way he does..." He dropped his head, digging his fingernails into the back of his neck in agony.

Scarlett's heart twisted as she watched his shoulders jerk, knowing he was crying beneath the shield of his arms. She used the moment of silence to absorb everything that had just happened. Owlen was her soulmate. *Their* soulmate. And he was leaving. The two people she loved more than anything were in pain... and she could stop it.

Scarlett gently stroked Finn's auburn hair. She leaned in close to him, pressing her lips to his ear. "I'll bring him back. I promise," she whispered, before giving his ear a gentle kiss. Her words struck him hard as Scarlett walked out the door. He uttered the same words before taking her life. *I'll bring you back. I promise.* And he failed. He dug his nails in deeper at the thought of Scarlett failing, causing blood to trickle down his hands.

Scarlett took a deep, calming breath as she made her way toward Owlen. She had no doubt where to find him, but as she approached the purple blooms, she found the familiar place completely transformed. A beautiful, majestic weeping willow tree awaited her, its branches reaching down like delicate fingers to caress the surrounding flowers.

As she stepped through the branches, a natural chandelier of light caught her attention. Scarlett's mouth fell open in wonder as thousands of fireflies fluttered among the branches, their tiny bodies twinkling like stars against the darkening sky.

She approached Owlen, who was standing beneath the willow facing the horizon, unable to look at her. "Owlen... it's beautiful," she whispered.

Owlen cleared his throat, trying to remain brave in the midst of his decision. "I wanted to give you something special before I go. Something to remember me, I suppose."

Scarlett wanted so badly to end this turmoil. To grab him, shake him, beg him to stay. But he was beyond that point. Done. She had to choose her words carefully, as if walking on eggshells, fearing the slightest misstep would shatter any chance of fixing things.

She stood closely behind him, clenching her fists to stop herself from reaching out to him. After careful contemplation, Scarlett broke the silence. "You know," she began casually. "there's something I never told you. Either of you." Owlen's head turned slightly in interest, so she continued.

"When I was... dead, I think I was somewhere in between here and Heaven. I don't know. It was dark. I couldn't see anything. I was terrified—and then I saw my parents."

"What?" Owlen turned to her, his eyes wide with surprise and concern. "Your parents? That must have been incredibly difficult."

"It was. They came to get me; they wanted me to go with them. I saw you and Finn also. Then everyone started fading and I was running out of time and I had to choose. So, I said goodbye to my parents and started running toward you both. I thought I was too late but you reached your hand out for me and I grabbed it. I guess that's when you brought me back, huh?"

Owlen gave a somber nod. "I'm so sorry. I didn't realize you had the choice to go with your parents."

Scarlett placed her hand on Owlen's arm when she saw the shame in his expression. "That's just it. Don't you see? I chose you. *Both* of you."

Owlen's face hardened slightly as he attempted not to let his hopeful emotions overcome him. "You chose your love for Finn and I understand that. You and I are great friends and I don't blame you in any way for your feelings. I would never want to stand in the way, so that's why I made my choice to leave."

"No, what you need to *understand* is that this is all new for me. This life, my powers, these feelings... for me it wasn't right to be with someone and have feelings for someone else. I thought I was doing something wrong. And I take responsibility for not being honest about how I feel, but you should too. And Finn."

Owlen shook his head. "I..."

"I know... you *can't*, right? You're afraid of what the truth might be? Finn is completely destroyed. I'm trying to hold it together and I *can't* do that either." She took a breath to calm the anger in her voice. "Just... just do one thing before you go. Please?"

As tears streamed from her amethyst eyes, Owlen looked away, unable to meet her gaze. "What's that?"

"Look into my mind. Or my soul... whatever. See for yourself. You owe me that at least." Owlen's eyes widened slightly as the fear set in. He opened his mouth to speak, but before he could refuse, Scarlett grabbed his hand and pulled it to her chest. "Please."

Owlen slowly met her gaze, his brow furrowed with worry. He gave a small nod and closed his eyes. Within a blink, he found himself inside her mind. It was a pleasant contrast from the dark cyclone of Finn's emotions.

Scarlett's thoughts floated past him like dandelion seeds in a gentle breeze. As he walked along, the path of memories and dreams resembled the very path he strolled to reach her purple flowers. Images of her parents floated by, far out of reach, while Finn's familiar crimson eyes were visible all around him. He searched for himself among the floating thoughts, but he was nowhere to be found.

Sadness set in as the absence of Owlen in her mind became real. A lump formed in his throat, and he began to regret agreeing to this torture. But just before he opened his eyes, something caught his attention. He stepped off the sunny path and into the shadows to investigate, and there he found them.

Thoughts of Owlen were hidden away like precious secrets, and he stepped forward, slowly, reluctant to intrude. For a moment he was looking at himself through Scarlett's eyes, and an electric shiver ran down his spine, igniting all of his senses.

Visions of his lips and eyes were floating around him. Glimpses of him that he didn't know were taken. He saw his fingertips gliding along the words of a book, then combing their way through her long, brown hair as her head rested on his lap. Owlen's eyes snapped open, wide with realization as he returned to Scarlett under the willow.

"Well?" She had only been waiting for a moment, but she hoped what he had seen was enough.

Owlen softened. Foolishness and shame formed as tears in his eyes as he spoke. "My dear, I'm so very sorry. I had no idea..."

"That I love you?" Without giving him a chance to respond, Scarlett reached up, grabbing the back of his neck, and pulled him toward her into a kiss. Owlen's entire body tensed as he felt Scarlett's soft lips against his own. Goose-bumps raced across his skin, and he had to blink to make sure he wasn't still within her mind.

His hand instinctively, yet gentlemanly, found its place at the small of her back, pulling her in tightly. Scarlett's fingers gripped his golden hair while her heart pounded in her chest at the feeling of his body against hers.

As their lips finally parted, they both drew a shaky breath, their eyes meeting in a silent understanding. Scarlett put her arms around his waist, pressing her cheek to his chest, happy to have fulfilled her promise to Finn. Owlen returned her embrace without reservation, the cloud of doubt lifted from his mind.

"I swear the two of you are going to give me gray hair, and I think we can all agree... I'm much too pretty for that." The two snapped from their embrace to see Finn approaching them with a smile. Scarlett and Owlen looked at each other with bemused glances before laughing.

"Good gracious! What happened to your neck?" Owlen stared wide-eyed at the dried blood that had made its way down to Finn's collarbone.

"Finn! Did you do that?" Scarlett's eyes were also fixed on the traces of blood staining his skin.

Finn's hand instinctively went to the back of his neck, where he felt the sting from his earlier bout with anxiety. "What, this? Just a scratch. More like an occupational hazard being a soulmate to you two." Finn wrapped his arms around them, drawing them into a tight embrace.

Owlen's eyes sparkled with gratitude as he leaned into the embrace, knowing Finn had forgiven him for the pain he had caused. Scarlett could feel the tension between them melt away as Finn's comforting arms surrounded them.

"Don't ever scare me like that again, angel," Finn whispered, his voice a mixture of affection and concern. He tightened his grip around Owlen, emphasizing the sincerity of his words.

Owlen squeezed Finn in return. The thought of leaving his friends seemed like a foolish memory now. "I promise."

# CHAPTER TWELVE

### IRON

Owlen stared at the plush bed that filled the small bedroom. It had remained untouched since he began spending his nights in the company of his friends. Decorative pillows were stacked neatly on top, leaning against the carved headboard. "What are you doing?" Scarlett asked, curiously, as she walked in.

"Well, with all the changes Finn made, I was thinking of turning this space into something else—something more useful. We don't really need a bed any more."

"You know, you could change the whole house if you wanted to. You could have a mansion or a palace with a wave of your hand." Scarlett had always been curious about Owlen's choice of such a humble abode.

"No, my dear," Owlen replied. "I much prefer a smaller, cozier home. I wanted our home to be a part of the beauty outside, not something that overshadows it. His eyes softened as he looked around, appreciating the intimate warmth of the space they shared.

Scarlett nodded sincerely as she approached the bed, her fingers trailing along the smooth, cool comforter. She sat down, feeling the soft give of the mattress beneath her. Sadness crossed her face as she looked at the bed, remembering the first night she slept in it as a mortal.

"I'll only change it if you want to, of course," Owlen quickly added, noticing her reaction.

Scarlett looked up at him, her expression softening. She patted the space next to her, motioning for him to sit beside her. Owlen hesitated for a moment, nerves fluttering in his chest, but then he crossed the room and joined her on the bed. The mattress dipped slightly under their weight, bringing them closer together.

Scarlett's fingers gently brushed Owlen's cheek as she guided his face toward hers. Their lips met in a slow, tender kiss. She pulled back slightly, her lips still brushing his. "A bed doesn't just have to be for sleeping," she said, her voice low and inviting. She grinned as she ran her fingers from his face down to his chest. Owlen's breath hitched as she gently pushed him back onto the mattress until he was lying beneath her. Her long chestnut hair lay all around him as she leaned over, her fingers teasingly lifting the hem of his shirt.

170

Owlen's hand quickly covered hers, his face flushing with nervousness. "I don't look like him, I'm afraid," he stammered, his blue eyes looking away shamefully as he pulled his shirt back down over his soft belly.

Scarlett turned his face toward hers, and placed her hand on top of his, which still rested on his stomach. "Trust me, you're absolutely perfect," she said, her voice filled with sincerity.

Before Owlen could respond, a familiar voice cut through the intimate moment. "See, I told you, angel!" Finn's words echoed from the living room, causing Owlen's face to grow even hotter.

The two started to sit up, their movements slightly awkward. Owlen stood up first, holding out his hand to help Scarlett to her feet before they made their way to the living room. Scarlett sat down on the floor in front of the fire, as Owlen joined Finn on the couch.

Owlen, realizing Finn was staring at him with a sly grin, could feel his porcelain skin growing red again. "What?"

"So I take it the bed stays?" he asked, with a chuckle, leaning back crossing his legs. "Or maybe we could use a *bigger* bed. What do you think?"

"Do you have to joke about *everything?*" Owlen muttered as he adjusted his collar. After a moment of regaining his composure, Owlen leaned closer to Finn, his voice a mere whisper. "You know, I've been watching her, and I really think she's ready," he said, his blue eyes fixed on Scarlett as she sat at the foot of the couch, not focused on their exchange. She was busy casting small balls of fire in her palm. Each flame danced and leapt gracefully into the fireplace, illuminating her face with warm, flickering light.

Finn knew exactly what Owlen meant. Traveling. The possibility of leaving the home they resigned themselves to for eternity. With the revelation that Scarlett was half-angel, the barriers of time and space no longer confined them. Finn watched her, intently, lost in thought. After a moment, he shook his head. "No, I don't think so."

Owlen's eyes widened slightly. "What do you mean? She's doing an amazing job with her powers. Traveling would be a breeze for her."

Scarlett, her heart suddenly pounding at the mention of the word, jumped up and hurried to the couch, squeezing in between them. "We can leave? Really?" Her amethyst eyes sparkled with excitement as she looked at Finn, but his face didn't mirror her enthusiasm. Instead, he shifted uncomfortably, moving away a bit.

"I don't think so," he repeated. He tried to mask the embarrassment and doubt in his voice.

Scarlett turned to Owlen, confused and disappointed. She grabbed his arm, placing his hand in her lap. "Why can't we? she asked him, searching his eyes for answers.

He paused for a moment, unsure how to address Finn's reluctance. He understood the love for their home, but the prospect of witnessing Scarlett's happiness as they showed her new places made his heart pound with excitement as well.

Glancing past Scarlett, Owlen focused on Finn. In a fleeting moment, he found his answers. Thoughts tangled with fears —*she could leave us, she could find somewhere or someone more exciting and realize she doesn't want to come back with us.* Even darker fears clouded his mind—concerns that Scarlett would want to return to her family and friends, which would only lead to heartbreak for everyone involved.

Owlen cleared his throat, determined to put Finn at ease. "Perhaps if we all agreed to some rules, we could give it a try?" He leaned forward, waiting for Finn's response. Scarlett leaned forward too, gripping Owlen's arm tightly, her eyes wide with anticipation.

Finn was silent for a moment. He looked into Owlen's kind eyes for reassurance. "What kind of rules?"

A smile spread across Owlen's face now that Finn was beginning to come around. He stood up, like a teacher about to impart on an important lesson. Scarlett watched him, focused on every word, her excitement barely contained. "Firstly," he began, his voice calm and authoritative, "we must *always* stay together. No one wanders off alone."

Scarlett nodded eagerly, her eyes flickering between Owlen and Finn. "Of course. We stay together."

"Secondly, we must never return to your timeline. It's far too risky to run into yourself, or anyone you may know, for that matter, and the complications it would cause could be catastrophic."

Scarlett's face fell a bit as she thought. But as she glanced at Finn, who was waiting on her response anxiously, she reached out, grabbing his hand. "I would never risk anything between the three of us. I agree." Finn let out a sigh of relief, slightly louder than he hoped, and he gave her an embarrassed smile, squeezing her hand.

"And finally, if for some reason either of us wants to return home, we *all* return together."

Scarlett's excitement bubbled over and she jumped up, wrapping her arms around Owlen. "This is perfect! I promise I'll follow the rules, I just want to do this with both of you."

Finn, still cautious, sighed and rubbed the back of his neck. "Fine. But the *moment* something feels off, we come straight back. Agreed?"

"Agreed," Owlen said, extending his hand. Finn shook it, reluctantly.

"Agreed!" Scarlett echoed, placing her hand on theirs.

Owlen beamed at them both, his heart swelling with relief and excitement. "Then it's settled. When should we begin?"

"Now!" Scarlett exclaimed. Owlen and Finn exchanged playful smiles.

"Okay, okay," Finn laughed. "You can have the first choice. Go on and pick a place. Remember, nothing from your own life, and we have to stay out of the way, so no putting us front and center of anything. Got it?"

Scarlett was caught off guard. She wasn't prepared to be the first to choose their location, and her mind drew a blank. She thought for a moment, concentrating carefully. "Got it," she said, finally. "Do I tell you what it is?"

"Maybe you'd better, just to make sure we all agree," Finn said.

"The horse race. Remember? You told me about it? Turning horses into crows, setting the barn on fire..."

"Of all the places we could go to, *that's* where you choose?" Finn asked with sarcastic disbelief, causing Owlen to chuckle.

Scarlett's face turned slightly red. "It's the first place that came to mind. Just to start with."

"Alright, I guess. Verdantville, home of the 1901 Emerald Run, coming right up. Does everyone agree?" Finn looked at his friends, both of whom nodded in agreement. "So it only takes one of us to guide the way, and as long as we're all connected, we'll all get there together. So hold hands," Finn instructed.

They all locked hands. Scarlett straightened up, not knowing what to expect. Owlen could sense her nerves and reassured her. "Remember, we'll be right beside you. You'll never be left alone. And if for some reason we're ever separated, just focus on coming back here. Your powers will work the same." Scarlett gave a small nod, taking a few deep breaths in preparation.

"Everyone ready?" Finn asked.

"We're ready," Owlen answered, squeezing Scarlett's hand tightly. With that, Finn blinked and their surroundings changed into a bustling scene. They found themselves behind the wooden grandstand, which was filled with rows upon rows of eager spectators. The stands were painted in a rich mahogany hue, and adorned with iron railings, adding elegance to the sturdy structure. The atmosphere was alive with anticipation and the murmur of excited voices.

Scarlett's mouth dropped open in wonder as she took in the sights. The women wore elaborate hats adorned with feathers and flowers, and their dresses were long and layered with lace and frills. She felt extremely underdressed, and took a step back to insure she stayed well hidden. *Next time I need better clothes,* she thought, not wanting to risk being seen changing her appearance. The men sported tailored suits with high collars and bowler hats, some puffing on cigars while chatting animatedly.

The air was filled with the rich scent of tobacco mingling with the aroma of various foods being sold by vendors. Their carts lined a pathway from the stands to the stables, offering a variety of treats. There were carts selling sausages, their spicy aroma wafting through the air, and others with the morning's fresh baked pastries. A popcorn vendor was busy scooping out fluffy, buttered popcorn into paper bags, while children waited eagerly in line for saltwater taffy, their coins in hand. Scarlett could hear the distant sound of sizzling and the occasional shout from the vendors.

Nearby, an announcer was shouting into a large, brass megaphone, his voice booming across the grounds. "Place your bets, ladies and gents! The betting booth is open!" Behind the counter, clerks were busy taking bets. Their hands worked quickly as they counted money and recorded each wager.

There was a large chalkboard behind him displaying the names of each of the twenty horses running in that day's race, and the odds for each horse. Top Billing was set to be the crowd favorite, with 3/1 odds, while Copper Coin was at the bottom with 60/1 odds. A line of eager betters stretched out from the booth, each person holding their money or slip, waiting their turn to place a bet.

Owlen, equally impressed by their surroundings, walked a few steps forward, easily fitting in with the dapper attire. He noticed a beautiful arrangement of flowers next to the track. They were planted in such a way that they spelled out *Emerald Run* in large vibrant letters. Each letter was a different color, creating a striking visual against the green grass of the track. Owlen's face lit up as he admired the display. "Oh, that's very clever," he remarked.

Finn heard the announcer's booming voice once more. "Last call to place your bets!"

He put his arms around his friends' shoulders, pulling them closer. "Spoiler alert—don't place any bets," he said, a sly grin crossing his face. "It won't be long now." He pointed to the large, white horse barn—a grand structure with a large, ornate wood carving of a running horse beautifully guarding the entrance. People were bustling in and out, their clothing a blend of practicality and finery, as they prepared the horses. Stable boys in flat caps and suspenders hurried about, while trainers gave last-minute instructions.

"See that?" Finn continued. "This is when I locked the stalls so the horses couldn't get out. They're probably trying to figure that out right about now. Once the smoke starts to fill the barn, the people will have no choice but to run out, leaving the horses inside. If you look *that* way, you should see the crows. Don't worry, everyone gets out just fine," he explained, his smug grin widening.

Scarlett's face lit up as she waited, eagerly. "I can't believe we're actually here."

Finn chuckled. "Just wait. The real fun is about to start."

People began to take their seats, filling up the wooden stands until they were brimming with spectators. Those who couldn't find a seat stood along the outside of the track, determined to have a good view of the race. The announcer's booming voice called for the riders to take their places.

The three friends stood behind the stands, their eyes fixed on the barn, waiting for the smoke that would signal the start of Finn's orchestrated spectacle. Unexpectedly, twenty horses exited the barn—one by one, their coats gleaming in the sunlight. They filed neatly into the starting gate, each rider adjusting their grip on the reins in preparation. Families of riders and owners followed, taking their place next to the track with a mix of excitement and nervousness.

Owlen and Scarlett exchanged confused glances, and then looked at Finn, who was staring at the barn with a furrowed brow. "Something's wrong."

"What do you mean? Should we leave?" Scarlett asked. Worry filled her eyes as she sensed the tension in Finn's voice.

Finn didn't answer. He kept his gaze fixed on the barn, waiting for the smoke that never came. "Where am I?" he asked himself, squinting his eyes to search through the crowd exiting the barn.

"Finn, are you certain we're at the right race?" Owlen asked. His own concern was growing as he tried to reconcile Finn's heroic tale with the unexpected turn of events.

"*Positive.*" Finn, ignoring his friends' concerned expressions, walked past them to get a better look at their surroundings. Owlen and Scarlett widened their eyes, taken aback by Finn's sudden indifference to being seen. He was focused, scanning the crowd and trying to pinpoint where his plan had gone wrong. His frustration was evident as he searched for any sign of his former self.

A gunshot rang out, singling the start of the race. The gates slammed open, and horses burst out in a flurry of motion. Iron shoes pounded the ground with a thunderous clatter. Riders leaned forward, urging more speed as the crowd erupted into wild cheers. The noise was deafening as the horses rushed past each other, jockeying for position.

Finn watched them closely, his crimson eyes narrowing as he followed the race with intense scrutiny. His mind raced as fast as the horses, thinking of his agreement to leave if something went wrong, but keeping his eyes locked, in search of answers.

As the horses rounded the track into the final stretch, a bolt of light pierced through the crowd, blasting a gigantic hole in the track. Chaos unfolded in an instant.

People screamed and ran in all directions, some pushing and shoving to escape, while others rushed forward to see what had happened. Owlen and Scarlett sprinted toward Finn with panic in their eyes. Scarlett wanted to help, but stopped, frozen with fear as she witnessed the mayhem before her.

"No! Get back, now!" Finn yelled to her. She turned back, taking her place safely behind the stands, feeling helpless as she watched the terror unfold.

 Owlen kept running toward the track. "Pardon me! Pardon me!" he yelled, pushing his way past the flood of people.

Horses couldn't stop in time as they approached the abyss. They whinnied in terror, their eyes rolling wildly as they tried to regain their footing. Riders shouted, desperately trying to control their mounts. The scene was a whirlwind of flailing limbs and tangled reins. They collided with each other, their momentum carrying them into the gaping hole.

Owlen waved his arms quickly, his movements fluid and precise. Horses and riders stopped midair, suspended above the chaos. Owlen placed them down safely alongside the track, like precious toys arranged with care.

Finn worked swiftly to mend the hole caused by dark magic. The ground began to seal itself, the edges drawing together under his power. His eyes flickered up occasionally, ensuring the crowd was out of harm's way. "Where's Scarlett?" he yelled over the lingering chaos.

"She's behind the stands! She's safe!" Owlen assured, his eyes scanning the crowd.

People were gathering their loved ones, running for the exit. Vendors abandoned their carts, rushing to the aid of the riders, shocked by what they just witnessed. Amidst the turmoil, nobody seemed to notice which heroes just saved the horses and their riders from certain death, and Finn was glad about that. He rushed to Scarlett, embracing her instantly. She clung to him, her breath ragged from adrenaline.

Meanwhile, Owlen was taking in the aftermath. His eyes roamed the scene, noting the scattered debris and horses being calmed by their riders. His heart sank when he realized the beautiful display of flowers had been trampled by panicked spectators. Petals were crushed and strewn through the grass. He glanced behind him, and with a discreet wave of his hand, he restored the flowers to their former glory, each petal and leaf returning to its rightful place. "That's better," he said proudly.

Before walking away, he noticed someone across the track, who looked oddly out of place. A very large muscular man stood like a statue, glaring at him, his chest heaving with anger. Owlen blinked, searching the man's dark thoughts.

A look of terror crossed Owlen's face as he watched the man disappear into thin air. He turned quickly, pushing and shoving through the exiting crowd. People jostled around him, confused and annoyed that he was going the wrong way. He burst through the mob, finally making his way behind the stands. His eyes scanned the area until he spotted his friends, completely unaware of what he had just witnessed.

He sprinted toward them, panting heavily, and without hesitation, he grabbed their arms. Finn and Scarlett looked up, startled by his sudden appearance, but before they could speak, the three disappeared, leaving the chaotic scene behind.

# CHAPTER THIRTEEN

### STEEL

Finn and Scarlett were both confused as to why Owlen pulled them home so quickly. Owlen was hunched over, in the throes of a panic attack, barely able to speak. "What's wrong with you, angel?" Finn put his hands on Owlen's shoulders, trying to meet his gaze.

Tears escaped Owlen's eyes as he struggled to calm himself enough to explain. "A man... demon... he did it... Morvina!"

Finn dropped his hands at the sound of her name, furrowing his brow. "Morvina? What'd she have to do with it?" Owlen was gasping, terror filling his eyes as he failed to form words.

Scarlett approached him with a worried look, placing her hands on his face. "Owlen, please calm down. What's wrong?" she pleaded, her eyes full of concern.

Owlen took a long, calming breath, trying to regain his composure. He removed his handkerchief and wiped his forehead. "There was a demon at the race. He was hired by Morvina. He took your place, somehow, doing the jobs you were assigned. Before he disappeared, I saw his thoughts." Pain filled Owlen's eyes as he continued. "He's a very dangerous, very powerful demon. He was told that if anything should go wrong, he was to skip to the very last job. The most *important* job." Owlen's eyes darted to Scarlett, and Finn instantly understood.

"Her?" Finn asked, nearly shouting.

"How can he do that? He can't come here, can he?" Scarlett asked, her eyes widening at the thought.

"Not you. The *old* you." Owlen's voice was trembling. "His plan is to take Finn's place the day he was supposed to kill you." Owlen looked at Finn with pleading eyes. "Morvina wants him to take her *alive.*"

"Then we get there first," Finn said.

"And we don't have much time," Owlen added. He embraced Scarlett, his expression serious. "He doesn't know your path that day, but *you* do. We'll need your help on that part." Scarlett gave him a small nod, understanding the gravity of what was about to happen.

Owlen straightened up, giving a quick run-down of the plan. "We agreed that returning to your timeline is strictly against the rules, but this situation is dire. You *must* understand that it's very important that we don't let your old self see us. Especially you. If anything throws off Finn arriving, then..."

"Then I won't be here?"

"Yes," Owlen answered, gravely. We must hurry. I need you to remember where you were *before* Finn reached you that day. He will most likely follow the exact timeline Finn did, but we can't be certain. We have to get there early just to be sure."

"I was painting." Scarlett searched her mind, trying to retrace steps that seemed like a lifetime ago. "Well, I was going to paint. When I woke up, I walked to the hardware store to buy supplies, then I walked home. That's it."

"Good. This will be much easier with you out of your apartment. Finn, you go to the hardware store to keep an eye on her, and make sure she gets back safely. It's too risky for Scarlett to be there. If you can, cause a distraction to slow things down a bit."

Finn thought about the plan carefully. "I can't leave her," he protested, his crimson eyes filled with worry.

Owlens tone softened, understanding his concern. "It's just for a little while. He wants the *mortal* Scarlett, and unfortunately, I'm no match for his dark magic. We need to make sure she is protected at the hardware store. The moment you know she is safe, come back to us. You'll be back before the demon shows up."

"And I'll *kill* him."

Owlen gave a small, knowing nod. "Is everyone ready?" he asked, hurriedly.

Scarlett and Finn exchanged glances. "Ready."

Owlen looked at Scarlett and took a deep breath. "Take us there, my dear."

They held hands as Scarlett concentrated deeply, pulling them into her world. The familiar surroundings of her apartment materialized around them—the unpainted walls, unpacked boxes, photos that flooded her mind with memories. But now was not the time to be sentimental.

Finn embraced Scarlett tightly, kissing her lips before pulling away. He turned to Owlen, hugging him tightly as well. "I'll be right back. Take care of her," he whispered. "If he shows up, *get out*." He gave them both a final wave before walking out the door.

Scarlett watched him from her window. "He can't use magic to get there?"

"He has to blend in as much as possible right now. If he's seen appearing out of thin air, it could be very costly."

The walk to the hardware store was longer than Finn had anticipated. He strolled through the door, trying to be inconspicuous, but the bell above the entrance rang loudly, alerting the elderly man behind the counter that there was a customer. "Good morning," the man said, slightly surprised by Finn's appearance.

"Good morning," Finn answered, turning away quickly to hide his crimson eyes. He walked into a nearby aisle, out of sight, and began his search for Scarlett. His heart raced as he navigated the narrow rows, his eyes darting from side to side. He avoided the few other customers, keeping his head down to avoid drawing attention to himself.

After several tense moments, he finally found her. Scarlett was in an aisle near the back, comparing rolls of painters tape. She was carefully reading the labels, oblivious to his presence. Finn's heart leapt at the sight of her. He slipped into the next aisle, peering through gaps between the shelves to watch her every move, feeling a mixture of relief and anxiety.

As he observed, he couldn't help but feel a pang of longing, resisting the urge to rush over and take her into his arms. There was an innocence about her. A fragility that made his chest tighten. It was strange to catch a glimpse of her life before the perilous fire that would change everything. His heart pounded as he savored these few moments, where she was untouched by danger and blissfully unaware of the chaos surrounding her present and future.

At the apartment, Scarlett and Owlen awaited Finn's return, tension thick in the air. "What happens if Finn can't stall her...or *me*, I guess. What if I get here before the demon does?"

"Finn and I have an understanding. If it comes to that, Finn wants you and I to return home, without him. It's the only option," he said solemnly.

Scarlett's face turned pale and Owlen approached her, wiping a tear from her cheek. "I have faith it won't come to that, though."

Hearing those familiar words made her feel relieved to have him by her side. "So, do you want to see some pictures while we wait?"

"I'd love to." Owlen smiled, welcoming the distraction.

Sacrlett approached the wobbly mantel, picking up the familiar Christmas photo from the group. A lump formed in her throat as she handed the photo to Owlen. "These are my parents, about four months before they died."

Owlen took the photo, examining it with a gentle smile. "They look very kind," he said, trying to offer some comfort. You look just like your mother—you definitely have her eyes."

"Thanks. People used to tell me that all the time. It bothered me for a while, but I miss it."

"There you are." A deep rumbling voice startled Owlen, causing him to drop the photo. The glass shattered with a crack. The two stepped back in fear as they realized the demon from the horse race was standing in the living room.

At the hardware store, Scarlett was walking toward the checkout counter, unaware of the danger unfolding at her apartment. Finn remained hidden in the shadows, ready to stall her. With a subtle motion of his hand, he caused the cash register to jam. The machine clunked loudly and let out a series of loud beeps.

The elderly man behind the counter was startled and looked down in confusion. He fiddled with the keys, trying to make sense of the abrupt malfunction. "I'm so sorry, miss," he apologized. "This darn thing seems to have jammed."

Scarlett gave him a warm smile, setting her supplies on the counter. "That's okay, I'm not in a hurry."

The old man returned her smile with a grateful nod and began to tinker with the cash register, his hands shaking slightly with nervousness. Finn watched from his hiding spot, relieved by Scarlett's willingness to wait. The man pressed buttons and jiggled the drawer, but it was clear he had no idea how to fix the problem. Finn knew he had bought some precious time. He took a deep breath, ready to spring into action the moment Scarlett left the store.

Owlen's voice shook but he stood his ground, trying to project bravery in his promise to protect Scarlett. "This isn't who you think it is," he said in a firm tone, despite the quiver. "You don't want her. Morvina wants a *mortal* girl."

Mordac's voice grew louder. "I know what she wants, and I ain't leaving without *her*," he snarled, spit dripping to the floor beneath him. His stench was suffocating, making it hard for them to breathe in the small room.

Owlen's thoughts raced as Finn's warning echoed in his mind: *If he shows up, get out.* The words were a dire command, a clear directive he wished he could ignore. The thought of leaving Finn alone to deal with this monster churned his stomach, but the reality before him was grim. With Scarlett clinging to his arm with a vice-like grip, he closed his eyes tightly, focusing intently on their home, to transport them away from their deadly situation.

Yet, his concentration faltered. The familiar pull of Luminara remained stubbornly out of reach, and when he opened his eyes, the unsettling sight above them confirmed his worst fears. The air was thick and churning, and a dome of dark magic was forming around them, sealing them in an impenetrable barrier.

"Leave," Owlen said, his voice strained as he kept his gaze fixed on the ominous figure. "You can get through... get out of here, now."

"No, I'm not leaving you," Scarlett insisted, shaking her head.

Owlen's heart ached at her determination. He slowly stepped in front of Scarlett, his body a shield. He was ready to protect her, despite knowing he could not match Mordac's dark magic. "You're not getting near her."

Scarlett's heart pounded in her chest. She felt cold sweat dripping down her back as she clung to Owlen, her fingers digging into his arm as she peered at the demon from behind him. Her breath came in shallow gasps. She pressed her forehead against Owlen's back, trying to draw some strength from his courage.

Mordac's fury erupted. His face twisted with rage as Owlen stood defiantly in his way. "You already ruined things *once*, you ain't doing it again!" he bellowed, lifting his hand. Electricity crackled, lighting up his palm like a torch, illuminating the room with a harsh, ominous glow. The air around him hummed with sinister energy.

Owlen stood his ground, his heart pounding as he closed his eyes, preparing himself for what he knew was coming. He could feel Scarlett trembling behind him. He grasped her hand and squeezed it tightly, offering her what little comfort he could in this moment. "I love you," he said softly. He took a deep breath, his last words heavy with emotion. "Please tell Finn, too."

The orb of electricity grew brighter, charging to a blinding flare, sparks flying out and sizzling on the floor. With a roar, Mordac thrust forward, releasing the bolt of lightning with deadly precision. The energy cracked through the air, shooting toward Owlen.

Scarlett's eyes squeezed shut in terror. She felt a pull from within herself, a surge of magic faster and more powerful than Mordac's blast. She pushed herself in front of Owlen, turning to face him, pulling herself close to him. From her back, two magnificent wings unfurled, with a sound of metal striking metal. Each feather was a gleaming piece of silver armor, forming a protective shield around them.

The bolt struck her wings with a deafening crack and deflected, ricocheting off the armored feathers. It rebounded with incredible force, heading straight for Mordac. The demon had no time to react. The bolt struck him square in the chest. With a final, anguished scream, his body disintegrated into dust.

The two opened their eyes, their breaths still heavy. The room was now eerily silent as they looked around the room, taking in the aftermath of the sudden battle. The only sign of the demon was a pile of settling ash where he stood just moments before.

Owlen looked at Scarlett, wide-eyed with awe and relief. He pulled her into a tight embrace, pressing his lips to hers. "Thank you so much," he whispered. "You saved my life."

Scarlett held onto him just as tightly, her body still trembling. The warmth of his embrace helped to steady her racing heart.

Owlen pulled back slightly, his eyes catching the glimmer of her silver wings. He took a moment to fully appreciate them. The sheen of each feather was perfectly crafted to offer beauty and protection. "They're just beautiful," he said, softly. "They suit you perfectly...just like a knight. You acted so bravely."

"You were going to risk your life for me, *you're* the brave one," she said, sincerely.

Finn appeared in the room with his usual swagger. "She's paying right now. I figured the old man suffered enough, so I finally helped him out. The demon should be here soon, then it's showtime." He blew on his knuckles, pretending to prepare for a fight, unaware of the events that just unfolded. He looked at his friends and stopped in his tracks. His brow furrowed as he took in the sight of Scarlett's wings and the ash that was still settling.

He moved closer, his eyes burning with worry and rage at the scene. "What happened?" he demanded.

"It's okay, we're fine," Scarlett assured him.

"He's dead," Owlen added, stepping forward. "Scarlett saved my life and killed him. She was just magnificent."

Finn gasped in disbelief, pulling them both into a tight embrace. "Why in the Hell didn't you leave?"

"We couldn't," Scarlett offered, before Owlen could answer, and reveal her refusal to leave without him. "He made a barrier, so we were stuck."

"I could have lost you both! I'm so sorry. I should have been here. Dammit!"

Scarlett hugged him back tightly. She could feel his heart pounding against her chest—a stark reminder of how close they were to losing everything. "It's alright. We're fine now."

"I'm so proud of you," he said, his eyes lingering on Scarlett's wings. He reached out, brushing his fingers against the metallic feathers. They were cool to the touch, yet he could feel power emanating from them. "Yours are almost as cool as mine," he smirked.

"Almost," she smiled. "So now that he's dead, will things happen like normal? I mean, you'll still be here to start the fire soon, right?"

"*And* save you," Finn replied. "As long as we're all gone before you get home, then everything will happen as it should."

They prepared themselves to leave, taking a quick look around to make sure they were leaving nothing behind. Finn was about to repair the broken picture frame, when he noticed something shiny buried within the small mound of ash, and he bent down to pick it up. "Look," he said, holding it up for them to see. "It's your bracelet."

Owlen's eyes widened with recognition. "Of course! That must be what he used to get here. I can't believe it wasn't destroyed."

Finn reached for Scarlett and put the broken chain around her wrist, but before he could mend it, she stopped him. "Wait," she said, gently. "I was so happy when I found this. I thought I lost it in the move. Leave it here for her to find. Please?"

Finn looked at her for a moment and gave her an understanding smile. "Alright," he said, softly. He walked back to the pile of ash and placed it on top, where it sank gently into its hiding place.

"Thank you."

Finn gave her a reassuring smile. "Let's get out of here," he said, wrapping his arm around her shoulders. "We have a timeline to keep." He walked over and glanced out the window. "Okay, you're heading this way now," he announced, turning back to Scarlett and Owlen. He positioned himself between them and grabbed their hands. "Is everyone ready?"

"Wait!" Scarlett suddenly let go of his hand and dashed to the window. Owlen and Finn watched her, exchanging worried glances. She stood there, her breath catching as she watched her former self walking up the sidewalk.

The young woman looked so innocent, so unaware of the trials she was about to face. Scarlett's heart ached with loss and protectiveness. She longed to run to her, to warn her, to protect her from the pain and terror that were to come. She had already been through so much. Her hand trembled as she pressed it against the glass, tears streaming down her face.

"Scarlett, my dear, we have to leave quickly," Owlen urged.

Finn gave her a worried look. His heart pounded as the fear of her not wanting to return was setting in. The thought of losing her again, even to her past, was unbearable. Owlen squeezed his hand, watching carefully as knots formed in his stomach. Scarlett took a deep, shaky breath. She watched herself for a moment longer, tears flowing freely. "Goodbye," she whispered. It was a farewell, not just to her former self, but to the world she had to leave behind without a chance for closure.

With a heavy heart, she turned away from the window and rejoined her friends. Her hand found Finn's, squeezing it tightly. "I had to see her," she said, looking up into Finn's eyes.

"I know," he replied. "If only she could see *you*. The woman you've become."

"She's in for quite the adventure," Owlen added. "She'd be so proud of you."

"You don't know what it means to me that you chose us. I know this is hard for you." Finn looked at her with grateful eyes.

Scarlett gave a small smile and glanced at the window. "She'll be fine. She'll have you both."

"And we'll love her dearly," Owlen replied, blinking away his tears. They savored a final moment before leaving Scarlett's life. They stood at the end of their journey, in the very place it began. A full circle.

"Are we ready?" Owlen asked, quietly, breaking the silence. Scarlett and Finn nodded, their hands reaching out to grasp his. "Alright, my friends... Let's go home."

# EPILOGUE

## END

The firm click of Morvina's heels cut through the quiet hallway. Her lips were pursed in annoyance since learning that Mordac had been killed, and her plan had failed. As she approached Soren's office, the doors opened on their own, revealing the imposing figure inside. "Come in, Morvina," his booming voice echoed through the office.

Morvina stepped inside. The door closed behind her with a thunderous clang. "So, you wanted to see me?" Morvina asked, crossing her arms.

Soren leaned back in his chair, tapping his leathery fingertips together. "I've been informed of some *interesting* developments," he said, coolly.

Morvina's heart skipped, but she forced herself to remain composed. Ultimately replacing Soren was meant to be a classified plan, and he had no idea how much information Soren knew, or *didn't* know. "I have no idea what you're referring to," she replied, her voice steady.

"You think I don't have eyes and ears everywhere? Even in the Labor Penitentiary?" His voice grew more menacing but he remained relaxed in his chair. "I received a memo from Bellamy."

"Bellamy's lying," she snapped, her irritation breaking through her facade. "You can't trust anything he says."

Soren's face darkened, and the fires around him roared to life, throwing giant, flickering shadows on the tapestries. "Don't insult my intelligence, Morvina. I know what you've been plotting. Going behind my back. Explain to me, exactly *what* were you planning on doing with me after you've taken my position?" he asked with a grin, barely visible beneath his cloak.

Morvina's annoyance flared. "It doesn't matter. Nothing is working like it was supposed to, anyway," she said, turning to leave. "Mordac is dead. There's nothing more to discuss."

"Wait a minute," Soren stopped her. "I have another memo here as well. One that might interest you." Morvina turned back slowly, raising her eyebrows. Soren picked up a parchment from his desk and unfolded it. "This one comes from *our* supervisors. It appears that the temporary ban on killing demons has been *lifted*."

Morvina's eyes widened with delight. Her sour lips formed a wicked smile. "That's great news!" she exclaimed, her mind already racing with possibilities. Thoughts of killing Finneas while Scarlett watched in horror, or perhaps the other way around. "This is *perfect*! I can finally get..."

Soren raised a hand, silencing her mid-sentence. The air around him crackled, and with a slight motion of his hand, Morvina was turned to dust, sending particles of ash into the air. He leaned forward, brushing her remains from his desk onto the floor. He picked up the parchment he read to her, looking down at its blank surface, and a smile stretched across his scaly face as he tossed it on top of her ashes.

# Acknowledgments

This is my first book ever! Thank you, my readers, for making it this far. Thank you for purchasing this book and giving this story a home on your physical or digital book-shelf. I hope you have enjoyed this lovely (no pun intended) journey and this wonderful world so far, and that you will keep reading until the end of the trilogy (I'll really appreciate it)!

Thank you to my developmental editor Fiona McLaren. You have helped me so much when it comes to worldbuilding and making sure my novel is concise. You are a wonderful teacher to me. In your feedback, you always highlighted parts that I have written beautifully. And parts that needed improvements, you brought it up in a professional manner and always suggested the best way for me to improve. Overall, you are the dream!

Thank you to my line-editor and proofreader Oskar Leonard. You did such a wonderful job taking care of all of the grammar errors in the book. You were patient and always quick to respond. Your suggestions have really brought my book to life, and made it ten times better!

Thank you to my cover and interior designer Michelle Connor (Etsy: ArtfulDigitalDloads). Thank you for creating the most stunning book cover. And you truly saved my life (or the life of my child—the book) by delivering this masterpiece in a timely manner. Seriously, the first-edition of my book would not be here without you!

Thank you, Grandma. This book is dedicated to you for a reason. You are the first person who believed in me. You are the first person to realize my passion for writing. You have been encouraging me to write a book since I was eight years old, long before I realized I could be an author at sixteen. I love you, and thank you for believing in my dreams at such a young age.

Thank you mom and your credit card. You paid for my editor and my cover designer to support my writing career. Thank you for supporting a small part of my journey.

Huge thank you to all of my Beta Readers. Honestly, you are the first people to read my book. You have seen it all—both the good and the bad. It's a good piece of blackmail, but thank you for sticking with me and providing me your honest opinions.

Lastly, I'm taking a few short sentences to thank my younger self (totally not cliché (note: it's my book lol). At the end of the day, we must believe ourselves first to make something a success. Thank you to my wonderful mind for crafting and thinking of these wonderful characters. Thank you to my younger self in grade seven for even considering writing a book. As your 'older-self' today—I appreciate you.

# ABOUT THE AUTHOR

M. L. Scarberry was born and raised in Ohio, where she still lives with her husband and daughter. From a young age, she found joy in creating pretend newspapers and writing short stories, always dreaming of becoming a published author. *Fallen Embers* is her debut novel, marking the fulfillment of that childhood dream. When she's not writing or working, she enjoys spending time at home with her family, or watching true crime documentaries.

www.ingramcontent.com/pod-product-compliance
Lightning Source LLC
Chambersburg PA
CBHW070658010826
48975CB00014B/2414